DEVIL'S MANHUNT

SELECTED FICTION WORKS BY
L. RON HUBBARD

FANTASY
The Case of the Friendly Corpse

Death's Deputy

Fear

The Ghoul

The Indigestible Triton

Slaves of Sleep & The Masters of Sleep

Typewriter in the Sky

The Ultimate Adventure

SCIENCE FICTION
Battlefield Earth

The Conquest of Space

The End Is Not Yet

Final Blackout

The Kilkenny Cats

The Kingslayer

The Mission Earth Dekalogy*

Ole Doc Methuselah

To the Stars

ADVENTURE
The Hell Job series

WESTERN
Buckskin Brigades

Empty Saddles

Guns of Mark Jardine

Hot Lead Payoff

A full list of L. Ron Hubbard's
novellas and short stories is provided at the back.

*Dekalogy—a group of ten volumes

L. RON HUBBARD

DEVIL'S MANHUNT

GALAXY
PRESS

Published by
Galaxy Press, LLC
7051 Hollywood Boulevard, Suite 200
Hollywood, CA 90028

Printed in the United States of America.

ISBN-10 1-59212-265-5
ISBN-13 978-1-59212-265-3

Library of Congress Control Number: 2007928464

CONTENTS

STORIES FROM PULP FICTION'S GOLDEN AGE

A ND it *was* a golden age.

The 1930s and 1940s were a vibrant, seminal time for a gigantic audience of eager readers, probably the largest per capita audience of readers in American history. The magazine racks were chock-full of publications with ragged trims, garish cover art, cheap brown pulp paper, low cover prices—and the most excitement you could hold in your hands.

"Pulp" magazines, named for their rough-cut, pulpwood paper, were a vehicle for more amazing tales than Scheherazade could have told in a million and one nights. Set apart from higher-class "slick" magazines, printed on fancy glossy paper with quality artwork and superior production values, the pulps were for the "rest of us," adventure story after adventure story for people who liked to *read*. Pulp fiction authors were no-holds-barred entertainers—real storytellers. They were more interested in a thrilling plot twist, a horrific villain or a white-knuckle adventure than they were in lavish prose or convoluted metaphors.

The sheer volume of tales released during this wondrous golden age remains unmatched in any other period of literary history—hundreds of thousands of published stories in over nine hundred different magazines. Some titles lasted only an issue or two; many magazines succumbed to paper shortages during World War II, while others endured for decades yet. Pulp fiction remains as a treasure trove of stories you can read, stories you can love, stories you can remember. The stories were driven by plot and character, with grand heroes, terrible villains, beautiful damsels (often in distress), diabolical plots, amazing places, breathless romances. The readers wanted to be taken beyond the mundane, to live adventures far removed from their ordinary lives—and the pulps rarely failed to deliver.

In that regard, pulp fiction stands in the tradition of all memorable literature. For as history has shown, good stories are much more than fancy prose. William Shakespeare, Charles Dickens, Jules Verne, Alexandre Dumas—many of the greatest literary figures wrote their fiction for the readers, not simply literary colleagues and academic admirers. And writers for pulp magazines were no exception. These publications reached an audience that dwarfed the circulations of today's short story magazines. Issues of the pulps were scooped up and read by over thirty million avid readers each month.

Because pulp fiction writers were often paid no more than a cent a word, they had to become prolific or starve. They also had to write aggressively. As Richard Kyle, publisher and editor of *Argosy*, the first and most long-lived of the pulps, so pointedly explained: "The pulp magazine writers, the best of them, worked for markets that did not write for critics or attempt to satisfy timid advertisers. Not having to answer to anyone other than their readers, they wrote about human beings on the edges of the unknown, in those new lands the future would explore. They wrote for what we would become, not for what we had already been."

Some of the more lasting names that graced the pulps include H. P. Lovecraft, Edgar Rice Burroughs, Robert E. Howard, Max Brand, Louis L'Amour, Elmore Leonard, Dashiell Hammett, Raymond Chandler, Erle Stanley Gardner, John D. MacDonald, Ray Bradbury, Isaac Asimov, Robert Heinlein—and, of course, L. Ron Hubbard.

In a word, he was among the most prolific and popular writers of the era. He was also the most enduring—hence this series—and certainly among the most legendary. It all began only months after he first tried his hand at fiction, with L. Ron Hubbard tales appearing in *Thrilling Adventures, Argosy, Five-Novels Monthly, Detective Fiction Weekly, Top-Notch, Texas Ranger, War Birds, Western Stories,* even *Romantic Range.* He could write on any subject, in any genre, from jungle explorers to deep-sea divers, from G-men and gangsters, cowboys and flying aces to mountain climbers, hard-boiled detectives and spies. But he really began to shine when he turned his talent to science fiction and fantasy of which he authored nearly fifty novels or novelettes to forever change the shape of those genres.

Following in the tradition of such famed authors as Herman Melville, Mark Twain, Jack London and Ernest Hemingway, Ron Hubbard actually lived adventures that his own characters would have admired—as an ethnologist among primitive tribes, as prospector and engineer in hostile climes, as a captain of vessels on four oceans. He even wrote a series of articles for *Argosy,* called "Hell Job," in which he lived and told of the most dangerous professions a man could put his hand to.

Finally, and just for good measure, he was also an accomplished photographer, artist, filmmaker, musician and educator. But he was first and foremost a *writer,* and that's the L. Ron Hubbard we come to know through the pages of this volume.

This library of Stories from the Golden Age presents the best of L. Ron Hubbard's fiction from the heyday of storytelling, the Golden Age of the pulp magazines. In these eighty volumes, readers are treated to a full banquet of 153 stories, a kaleidoscope of tales representing every imaginable genre: science fiction, fantasy, western, mystery, thriller, horror, even romance—action of all kinds and in all places.

Because the pulps themselves were printed on such inexpensive paper with high acid content, issues were not meant to endure. As the years go by, the original issues of every pulp from *Argosy* through *Zeppelin Stories* continue crumbling into brittle, brown dust. This library preserves the L. Ron Hubbard tales from that era, presented with a distinctive look that brings back the nostalgic flavor of those times.

L. Ron Hubbard's Stories from the Golden Age has something for every taste, every reader. These tales will return you to a time when fiction was good clean entertainment and the most fun a kid could have on a rainy afternoon or the best thing an adult could enjoy after a long day at work.

Pick up a volume, and remember what reading is supposed to be all about. Remember curling up with a *great story.*

—Kevin J. Anderson

KEVIN J. ANDERSON *is the author of more than ninety critically acclaimed works of speculative fiction, including The Saga of Seven Suns, the continuation of the Dune Chronicles with Brian Herbert, and his* New York Times *bestselling novelization of L. Ron Hubbard's* Ai! Pedrito!

DEVIL'S MANHUNT

CHAPTER ONE

DESPERATION PEAK rises green out of six thousand square miles of parched Arizona desert, a deceptive and deadly lure. It has game, streams and gold—but it also has an entire barricade around it, an unbroken ring of white alkali deserts, burning and acrid, waterless and uncrossable at any but the coolest season of the year.

Thus protected, Desperation Peak long retained its treasure; like an emerald set in the center of hell, the price was high for its taking.

Tim Beckdolt had nearly died braving the pitiless wastes, but his adventure had been rewarded. Once across the alkali sinks he had reached the tumbled canyons, clear springs and wooded slopes of the peak. He had lived on venison until his cartridges had all been used. Then he had kept his soul encased with body by snaring rabbits and birds. He had worked and wandered alone in this virgin desert-isolated fastness for eight months before he had found the rich placer. He had no salt and no flour. His clothing was a ruin of faded ribbons and he needed many things to work a claim. But to undertake another trip across the sinks, and return, particularly at this season of the year, was unthinkable; even his jenny had died of the privations endured in coming here.

Tim Beckdolt did not ask questions of himself as to how he would get it out. From the moment he struck it, all his attention was for the gold. In two or three months it would rain, then he would leave. Until then he was a castaway, clinging to an island upon a scorching sea. He would cache his wealth and leave it to await his return, would bring back a mule train to take it outside.

The discovery of this ancient creek bed was such that three months of labor had netted him slightly in excess of a hundred and seventy-five thousand dollars. A few more weeks of work would exhaust the placer; then he would rest and wait for the November rains so that he could leave.

At fourteen, Tim had gone wandering across the West as a boy of all work, under the most indifferent masters, a runaway from a home that wouldn't have him. He had learned prospecting in two heartbreaking years under the absolute tyranny of old Scotty O'Rourke—who had outlived three partners and had tried to outlive Tim. The world-weary youngster now saw himself as a successful young man; he wanted a ranch of his own, fine horses to ride, and the wherewithal to influence the unkind.

At twenty-three he had it all within his grasp. Now and then he would straighten up, limber his back and gaze ahead of him. But he was not seeing red rocks and pines; he was seeing ranch houses, thousands of cattle grazing, white horse fences and himself in fine clothes. It was an innocent dream.

At four o'clock on the afternoon of July 13, it was shattered entirely and utterly.

A shadow fell across his sluice and Tim stopped, not looking back, but staring at the reflection in the cold blue gleam of a Winchester barrel.

The first words he heard bit deep. They were indifferently, even wearily, spoken. "Wait a minute, Sven, don't kill him."

Tim held on to the sluice box to keep his hands from shaking. He turned carefully until he stood leaning against the rough, hard slabs, water curling around his ankles, sweat growing cold on his face. The man called Sven was rendered even more huge by his standing on the bank two feet higher than the water.

He was shaggy, with matted hair; his clothes were nondescript and slovenly. His face was big, with small eyes.

The other man was seated on a rock. He was young, handsome, about twenty-eight and dressed in neat corduroy.

"I don't know how you feel about it, Sven," he said, "but I've no taste for the muck and moil in the July sun. There are a few thousands yet in the gravel pile and our friend here appears to be a willing worker. Aren't you, son?"

Sven grunted and lowered the end of the Winchester to the ground. It looked like a small stick in his hand, and the big pistol which girded him was a toy against the hugeness of his thigh.

"Don't let us interrupt your work, my friend," said the young man.

"How did you make it across the sinks?" said Tim.

"Why, as to that, there are two men who didn't—two men and a mule." He laughed quietly and looked at his gun.

Tim saw the extra canteen which was slung about Sven, and knew with an abrupt insight why the two were not here.

"A pleasant place," said the young man. "I dare say that you have had all this peak with its foothills to yourself. Looks like there is game. I told you there would be game, Sven. Something to eat. Something to kill."

"You vant Aye should shoot some meat, Mr. Bonnet? Or you vant to hunt it again?"

"Seen any mountain lion or bear up here, my young friend?"

Tim looked from Bonnet to Sven. Something of the terror of his situation was coming clear to him, turning his stomach like ground glass.

"Our young friend here doesn't seem to be of much help as a hunting guide. Supposing you step out there, Sven, and take a bead on a potential banquet. If you see any bear or puma, or anything worthwhile, let me know."

Bonnet did not bother to aim a weapon. He had already possessed himself of the rifle that had been in Tim's camp and had loaded it. He let it lie unnoticed at his feet.

Tim looked at the rifle and at the far bank. A crooked, almost hopeful smile appeared faintly on Bonnet's face. He hitched himself back a few feet from the rifle. His tongue caressed his parched lips. Tim was cold inside. Bonnet hitched himself further away from the weapon, and his smile grew, showing even, perfect teeth.

Bonnet reached inside his coat and brought out a short gun which he tossed down the bank so that it lay only a little further from Tim than the rifle was from Bonnet.

Tim's fingernails were sinking into the sluice. He could envision himself lunging forward and grabbing the gun, could see Bonnet snatching at the rifle. He tried desperately to anticipate the outcome, crouched a little lower.

Suddenly Tim sprang up the bank, sweeping the Smith & Wesson into his grasp and leveling it. With some astonishment he saw that Bonnet had not moved but stood looking with bright eyes upon Tim. The Smith & Wesson's hammer fell on an empty chamber, then another—another, another, another and another.

Bonnet picked up the rifle, jacked the shell into its chamber and laid the weapon across his knees. "Throw the gun here, young man. In a few days, when you have all the gold out of that gravel and neatly sacked, you and I may yet entertain ourselves with a little sport." He laughed quietly.

Tim worked methodically after that, worked day after day, through days beyond his counting. The water swirled about his knees, the heavy gumbo moved to the riffles; he cleaned out the rocks, cleared the tailings, all in the mechanical fashion of a sleep-walker. His hands bled, his limbs ached; and as he worked hopelessness gripped him.

He had not realized until now the part his stepfather had played in the joy of his discovery. The idea of sending his mother beautiful clothes, hiring help for her, seeing to it that his younger sister received an education and escaped the miseries of a farm drudge had occupied, unbeknownst to him, the highest position in his plans. Now his stepfather could go on saying, "That no-good young pup. Knowed he'd never amount to nothin'. Skinned out and never bothered to write you a letter. Told you he was no good, Samantha. I done plumb right, tryin' to beat him into line." And his mother would have no answer, not now; she wouldn't be able to call his stepfather's attention to the beautiful ranch her son owned, to the fine horses he rode, to the high and influential friends he had. She could think, maybe, that something terrible had happened to him which prevented him from ever writing, but she would not know.

His captors paid very little attention to him. By day, one or the other of them would sit with rifle nearby and lazily watch Tim's labors, prodding him on when he slowed. At meal times they would toss him chunks of meat; at night they would lash his hands and feet together and tie him to a stump to save themselves the tedium of watching him. At dawn he would awaken, his extremities blackened by choked circulation; he would lie waiting to be loosened while Sven snored swinishly, close by his side.

Tim did not realize how little he regarded Sven as a man. It was like being in captivity with a wild animal. Sven's body odor, the matted hair, the bestial bluntness of his face, the grunts with which he spoke, all added into a likeness to a wild brute. The illusion was strongest when Sven ate. He tore the joints of venison apart with his bare hands and, thrusting his face into the half-cooked flesh, would snuffle and tear and grind with a whining satisfaction which, Tim thought, would have been more complete if the meat had been alive.

Bonnet did the hunting. Sven did all the work with slavish deference, even bringing in what Bonnet had shot. The game was usually a doe or a fawn. It always had been wounded once and then shot between the eyes. Always wounded. The meat was sometimes rank with the fear taste which comes when an animal, not instantly killed, lies in terror and agony before dying. The wounding holes were always in painful places.

On one such hunt Bonnet was gone all morning. About eleven o'clock, before the sun fell across the sluice and lighted the gold in the riffles, a series of six shots was heard. Sven started up alarmed. After a long interval there was a seventh. When Bonnet returned, his shoulder was scratched and his coat torn. He was not bored then; he was excited. There was something like honesty in his laugh when he turned Sven back.

"No, no game," he said. "It was a bear. A big one. Had an eight-foot scratch mark. I tracked him for two hours before I found him, and he had my wind before I came up. Oho, he was mad. He reared and charged and I barely had time to shoot. Hit him five times and the brute was *still* alive when he came up to me. Oh, he was mad, let me tell you. I caught him six times all in the throat and chest. He was spitting and roaring like a drunk in a barroom. This blood's all his; I wrestled him for a minute or more before I could get my gun away. I let him have the last one right in the roof of the mouth. Oh, he was a rough one, he was.

"Ah," and Bonnet stretched. "I haven't enjoyed myself so much since my dear old mother's funeral."

All the remainder of the day Bonnet was in extra good humor; he even told Tim to knock off for a while and rest himself, offered Tim some tobacco. Once in a while Bonnet chuckled in a satisfied way. He would poke Sven playfully and laugh.

"You should have seen him," he told Sven late in the afternoon. "An eight-foot scratch mark. I saw them on the trees. Big as you, almost, and all fight." He paused and looked speculatively at Sven. "Too bad you're so valuable to me." He slapped Sven resoundingly on the shoulder, playfully cuffed his ear. "What a game you'd make, my Swedish friend. And what a trophy! I'd mount your head on a silver board up above the fireplace. That I would!"

Sven turned quickly away and began to stir up the fire; there was a gray look under his beard.

After the incident of the bear, his own approaching fate seemed all the more terrible to Tim. Night after night he would struggle with his bonds until his wrists and ankles bled, but never once could he slack those ropes.

Daily, the pile of gravel grew less. Tim saw, with something like a shock one morning, that only a few hours of labor would be left. He took his pick and went savagely into the gravel vein. But there was only red clay there, all the blue was gone. He thought of breaking the sluice but he realized that the three or four hundred dollars remaining to be washed would be of no account to Bonnet. He could do nothing else but dawdle over his work now, buying a few hours of life with a few pounds of muck. It never occurred to him otherwise than that Bonnet would kill him as soon as the work was finished, kill him, cave a bank in on him and take the gold away.

Tim worked as slowly as he could and was only occasionally prodded on by the watchful young man. At noon Sven roasted a haunch of venison and they ate, Tim seated by the sluice.

Two or three times Tim glanced up and surprised Bonnet looking at him. He was amazed to be given an extra slab of meat.

"Eat hearty," said Bonnet. "In the name of the ancestral halls of Virginia which raised me, I never permit a guest to go hungry." He laughed, and his strange eyes flickered at Sven. "You never knew, I suppose, what a hope of the house I was. Yes sir, my old mammy was sure her Stede would be a great man someday, and the governor and the old lady built a mighty high castle of hopes. The world was mine—fast horses and faster women. A hunt before breakfast and a duel before dark. Ah yes, that was the life—all bows, poetry, soft music, tradition, silver and old lace. They thought it was enough to hold me. Their idea of a great man was the overlord of a few dozen slaves. Hah!" He looked fixedly at the slice of dripping meat in his hand.

Suddenly his face changed. He pitched the meat violently into the dirt. "Shut up! Shut up! Shut up! Damn you!" He stabbed the meat with his hunting knife, stabbed again and again until the knife flew from his grasp. His face was livid with rage. Sven cowered.

Bonnet stood suddenly and grasped his rifle. For a minute Tim was certain that he was going to be shot. Mr. Bonnet strode off and was soon vanished from sight.

Sven huddled beside the fire, shivering. Tim sat where he was, looking wonderingly at the piece of meat in the dust. As time progressed, Sven became more and more nervous.

He looked now and then accusingly at Tim as though Tim had done something to offend his master. At last Sven rose,

11

undecided, but determined to do something about it. He picked up the revolver and fired it three times into the air. There was no answer from Bonnet.

The trees and the grass of Desperation Peak whispered in the afternoon wind. Sven's agitation increased, he would raise his nose to the wind and, with a sudden surge of hope, sniff worriedly. Finally he beckoned Tim to come up to the camp spot. Tim went. He found himself seized and trussed to a log, and he carefully did not resist. Sven hastily picked up a rifle then and disappeared.

A strange exultation shook Tim. All the time that Sven had been lashing him he had carefully tensed his muscles and held his arms out a small distance from his body. By relaxing now, his bonds were loosed; the exultation was mingled with terror lest Bonnet should return before he could get entirely free.

CHAPTER TWO

I N less than five seconds after Sven had vanished in the
trees, Tim had one hand out, in another fifteen seconds he
had both hands loose. The remaining coils of rope, enlarged,
fell about his ankles and he feverishly tore at the knots which
were all that remained between him and liberty. He sprang at
the pile of effects which lay near Bonnet's rough bed, hunting
for a weapon. All he found was a short sheath knife. He
turned to grab a canteen but at that moment a rustling in the
pine needles on the slope started him up like a frightened
rabbit. He raced across the creek and up the far bank to dive
out of sight in a clump of alder.

He flung himself headlong through the brush. The thickets
tore at his hands and clothes. Roots tripped him and he slid
over slippery pine needles, more than once losing his balance,
bringing up with a bruising crash against a tree. He passed
half a dozen gullies before he stayed the haste of his flight.

A quarter of a mile lay between him and camp. He turned
at right angles and went scurrying up a wash where, from
boulder to boulder, he could find cover. He came at last to
a prominence from which he could look back over his trail.
The forests and meadows over which he had come remained
innocent of pursuit so far as he could see. There was a beating
in his throat.

13

Temporarily satisfied that he was not immediately pursued, Tim turned to gaze out across the sinks. He saw them shattering the sunlight, parched and deathly, between himself and freedom. It came to him then that he was in a second kind of trap. Not for months would rain come and only rain would make it possible to cross those wastes without a canteen.

His heart began to race. He looked up above him to the towering heights of Desperation Peak. Then a kind of calmness came to him, for he realized that this was wilderness; in its tumbled, folded terrain were thousands upon thousands of hiding places from which one could reach water.

Then he stared back along his trail and saw something moving on a meadow. It was Sven.

The big Swede came along at a trot, his eyes fixed on the earth, his course a zigzag which picked up all the signs of Tim's spoor. Behind him at a considerable distance walked Bonnet. The young man's gun was carelessly cradled over his arm; his hands were in his pockets, his gait was a saunter, as though he took the utmost joy in the song of the birds about him.

Tim drew back. He scurried down from the prominence, took one final glance at the far-off meadow and scuttled on up the ravine. He ran for a mile, keeping on rocks where he could. Now and then he slipped off into the wet sand. When he found a stone ledge he cut from one ravine to the next. He kept on rising, attempting to keep as high as he could so that he could always command his back trail.

At last he reached an eminence and looked back. Sven appeared on a ridge and studied the mass of boulders ahead.

Now and then Sven would turn and glance back, as though waiting. After a little, Bonnet wandered up, gun in the crook of his arm, and spoke for a while with Sven; then Bonnet took something out of his pocket, something which flashed in the afternoon sun. It was a pocket spyglass. Tim ducked, shivering.

When he looked up again Bonnet had put away the pocket telescope. He sat now doing something which Tim could not make out. Sven came back into view carrying a stick which he fixed in the ground. A moment later a tiny speck of white was fluttering from the top of it. Ostentatiously then, Bonnet and Sven walked down the ridge, returning toward camp, which lay some distance straight down. Tim had doubled his tracks and cut back higher but even with the camp.

The two walked, keeping in sight. They were soon far away in this distance-deceptive air; Bonnet then seated himself and Sven stretched out.

For a long time Tim remained where he was. At length he crawled out and started toward the stick.

Now and then he stopped, looking intently down the mountain at Bonnet and Sven. Halfway to his goal he halted, apprehensive of a sudden sprint by Bonnet or Sven to catch him.

He reached the stick and took the note.

> I don't know why you ran away. I meant nothing but good by you, but now that you are gone I see no chance of persuading you to come back. You do me the disservice of distrusting me. You cannot live long without food. And eventually we shall catch you.

If you do want to come back, walk down the ridge toward us. I don't suppose that you will. By the way, you lay a very good track. Even Sven, who has a nose like a fox, had difficulty following it. I didn't expect you'd be so clever. Good sport, what?

Mr. Bonnet

Tim looked down the slope at the two motionless figures. He began to tremble as he recalled what Bonnet had said about mounting Sven's head.

He ripped the note across, and turned to look up into the heights of the mountain.

A bullet nearly got him. He ducked from its spiteful snap, before the report reached him he had flung himself into the gravel. By hard running, Bonnet had come within five hundred yards of him, was starting up now to come nearer.

Tim sprang up and the rifle puffed smoke. Racing over the flats, bounding over logs, ducking through trees, Tim wildly attempted to place distance between himself and his pursuer. He plunged through a creek and hauled himself to a bench. Somewhere ahead he heard another stream roaring. He darted toward it, pausing only once upon the bank to look back. There came Bonnet about six hundred yards behind him, traveling in a straight line, his run effortless.

Tim started to plunge into the stream, then saw above him that, amongst its cascades, a pinnacle of rock raised itself. A moment later he was resting on top of that pinnacle, was out of sight from the stream. He breathed heavily and hoarsely, waiting for Bonnet.

*Racing over the flats, bounding over logs, ducking through trees,
Tim wildly attempted to place distance between
himself and his pursuer.*

The young man came to the edge of the water and looked up and down it. He was hardly winded. He looked to the load in his rifle and then started upstream, walking through the swift water of the cascade, coming closer and closer. In a moment now he would be directly under the pinnacle.

Tim took a ten-pound rock and held it securely; he waited, gauged his distance, then, looking down on the corduroy shoulders only a few feet distant, drove the boulder hard against them.

The movement of the water baffled his aim, and the blow was only a glancing one; before he could take up a second missile, Bonnet, falling sideways and rolling, had found cover under the overhanging branches of an alder. The rifle lay in the swift water. Tim was on the verge of leaping down after it when the spiteful crack of a pistol sent rock chips flying near his head. He ducked back.

"Aha," said Mr. Bonnet. "Why, there's more life and fight in you than I had thought. This *is* sport. But here, it isn't fair; you haven't any weapons. Look, down on the bank where you entered the stream I will lay a sheath knife. It is long and sharp and will come in handy. Yes, and I will even put a packet of dried meat there, since there is no fun in hunting starving game. It's a free gift." There was a rustle in the bushes.

Tim lay still. He was afraid to wait long, afraid of being encircled. He came up cautiously. A second shot knifed splinters from the rock.

But Tim, having risked it, flung himself backwards and

down. He lit on the far bank. A third shot plowed mud at his feet. He ducked into the trees. Behind him he heard Bonnet yelling.

"Fair enough. Fair enough! No hard feelings! Come back for the meat! I'm going back to find Sven!"

Tim cut at right angles and came into position where he could see the stream clearly. Bonnet was retrieving his rifle and beating the water out of his hat. As good as his word, he went back to the bank, placed the knife and the food there. He sauntered off across the meadow, disappearing a few minutes later amongst the trees, eight hundred yards away.

Tim took a deep breath; he dived out of his cover, splashed through the stream and scooped up the packages.

Instantly he sensed motion and leaped aside. One of Sven's hands barely touched him, and Tim was away again, through the water and up the bank. He glanced back once. Sven was shaking his head groggily, trying to swing around and start his bulk in immediate pursuit.

Tim stretched out a lead of a hundred and fifty yards and carefully maintained it. He eased every time that Sven eased, until they both were traveling at a dogtrot. The country here was steeper and sharper, with fewer trees and more rocky knife-backs.

Tim went straight ahead for some distance. He crossed each successive rise and continued on in a straight line. Then, on the final rise, he turned sharply downhill, leaped from boulder to boulder and dived out of sight in some brush.

He lay still, waiting.

Sven stopped at the top and stared. He looked up the gully and then down it, sniffed like a bloodhound, lifting his head and opening his mouth to flavor the wind. He grunted and went cautiously up the slope.

He worked his way some distance up the gully and then turned back. Warily he eyed the thickets before him, took out his revolver and checked the load. He got down on his hands and knees to peer under the bushes.

Tim's hand was sweaty on the knife. He released it for a minute and wiped his palm on his pants, grasping the weapon anew.

Sven ducked back and forth. He sniffed and grunted with the effort of kneeling. At length he crept back and looked at the clump of bushes. His small animal eyes traced out the telltale pattern of snapped twigs. Suddenly he stood up.

"Aye vas see you," he said. "You coom out."

He waited then.

Tim, not breathing, watched the swinging muzzle of the revolver.

"Aye vas cooming in," said Sven, but he did not move; the revolver continued to swing in a slow arc back and forth across the brush.

For nearly an hour Sven stood there, waiting, sniffing, listening.

Tim carefully began to strip the twigs from a slender sapling which rose beside him. Once he made a noise.

Sven was instantly on the alert. "You coom out," he bellowed. "Aye vas tired vaiting."

Tim carefully inserted the knife through the center of the

20

wood, driving it with short jabs until four inches of it protruded from the far side. It was Bonnet's knife, sharp, pointed, thin, deadly. Tim checked his ground again. The course of twigs lay along the only obvious opening into the thicket. The knife was pointed in that direction.

Gently Tim brought the sapling back. With the slender top of the sapling, he took himself some distance from where he had been.

"Mr. Bonnet," yelled Sven. "Coom up, Mr. Bonnet. Oooh, Mr. Bonnet, coom up."

Tim took a creeper and wrapped it carefully around the bottom of the bush near the knife, then backed off again.

"Coom up, Mr. Bonnet," cried Sven.

Tim backed up, holding on to the creeper with one hand, bending the sapling into a steep bow with the other. He burrowed into the earth. With a slow pull he caused the bush to bend some distance from him. The instant reply was a shot. A patter of torn twigs and ripped leaves filtered down into the underbrush. Tim gave the bush a violent jerk. Two more shots followed. He pulled the springy growth toward him and then let go. Three shots tore through the brush and the last severed the creeper which Tim had used for his decoy position.

Sven came blundering ahead, tearing up shrubs and breaking small saplings as he followed the previously broken twigs into the tangle. He was grunting and snuffling, fending the bushes away from his face.

"Aye vas got you now, you bet," grunted Sven.

Tim's grip on the top of the sapling tightened. The knife

21

glittered wickedly. Pressed close to the earth, he gauged his distance carefully. He waited until Sven was nearly at the sapling's base and then let go.

The knife flashed in a short arc. The thin, wicked point thunked into Sven's flesh. Sven, with a howl of pain, lurched to tear himself free from the small trunk. His finger convulsed on the trigger and the hammer struck an empty cartridge.

Tim, the second knife held tight, leaped forward. He gripped the blade as a rigid extension of his arm, drove so hard that his hand sank into the soft flesh of Sven's abdomen. The Colt slapped down and caught Tim across the forehead. The world was curtained from him by a swift cascade of blood. He stumbled backward, feeling the air moving under the powerful drives of Sven's avenging arms. Tim tripped.

He rolled backward through the thicket, torn by twigs, clawing at his eyes to get them free of the hot slippery flow of his own blood. The wild animal smell of Sven beat against him in waves. Something struck against his foot and moved, then there was silence.

Tim cleared his vision and drew backward. At his feet lay Sven, breathing heavily. His shirt and side were torn by the first knife; the hilt of the second still protruded from his stomach.

Tim started to wriggle away, thought better of it and approached his fallen enemy. He wrestled the second knife out of the stomach and wrenched the first from the tree. The sweet smell of crushed greenery was heavy in the thicket, stronger than Sven's stench or the salty odor of new blood. Sven's breath came in hoarse gasps.

Shaking with anxiety lest Bonnet come up, Tim worked himself out of the thicket. He shortly emerged from the far side of it, his clothing torn, his face a caked mass. He clawed his way up the side of the ravine.

Tim vaulted the ridge and slid down the far side. He turned quickly up this ravine and in a few minutes was zigzagging amongst boulders. He was headed toward a grove of tall sighing pines. He ran noiselessly over the mat of dead needles. The sough of trees covered the slight noise of his going.

CHAPTER THREE

NIGHT found him hidden and panting. He was between two rocks, voraciously gnawing at the packet of dried meat that Bonnet had furnished.

He had eaten the packet of food halfway before he felt nausea; it was not an immediate thing and he attributed it to the starvation he had suffered. But when he took his next bite he realized that there was a metallic taste to the meat which should not be there. He chewed it experimentally, then the vision of Mr. Bonnet's eyes glittered before him. In a sudden suspicion he looked at the meat.

It was a piece of venison and it had expertly been slit through the center. Laying it open, he found tiny granules of a white something. He had only just started into the area.

Tim was a mining man; he was too well trained by his hard old master not to recognize arsenic when he saw it.

At first he could not lose what he had eaten, so starved and shrunken was his stomach. Then, when he finally managed it, the raw tissues of his stomach and throat lining churned into one spinning agony. He lay half-fainted and gasping on the rocks.

About midnight he was able to drag himself to water and rinse his stomach. After that he crawled painfully upwards into the cliffs where hunger waited but where no man could track.

For three days Tim huddled amongst the crags, dazed and sick. But when his illness passed his hunger returned and all one morning he lay watching game on the lower slopes. The sight of it maddened him; debating his course for hours, he at last succumbed.

Slowly, watchfully, he crept from the heights, down the cliffs and into the green meadows.

He tried to make a snare but could not, so badly were his hands shaking. The squirrels and the birds mocked him and he wandered here and there, watchful for pursuit but more watchful for his food. Dried grass would not stay his hunger.

At about five o'clock, knife in hand, he began to trail a rabbit. The rabbit would hop a few paces then turn to look back to the man who followed him. When Tim approached, the rabbit would hop further, sit up again and wait, curious.

For about an hour Tim gave no attention whatever to his immediate whereabouts. The rabbit would run off a short distance and wait. Tim would follow on, hoping to get within knife-throwing distance.

Ahead were two large boulders crouched on the slope. Some hidden sense, clarified by his hunger-attuned mind, caused him to look toward the rocks. It was a very small spot of reflected light, but the sun was glancing there from a gun barrel! He was within four hundred yards!

The rabbit was in a slight gully, out of sight now from the rocks. Tim, pretending that his game had gone elsewhere, continued to go through the same evolutions as before, stopping and creeping on as though he still hunted his game. He turned his course at right angles and insensibly drifted lower on the slope toward the stand of pines.

Tim even slowed his pace, his spine crawling as though it already felt the impact of a Winchester's soft-nosed slug. He dropped on all fours as though to examine tracks on the ground. The rabbit had vanished some time since, but such was the terrain that the rifleman would not be able to see this. Once or twice Tim even started back toward the rocks for a few yards to raise the hope for a certain and easy shot at him.

It was very hot. He was near the base of Desperation Peak. A quarter of a mile below and away, the alkali sink stretched out like a white-hot frying pan. Heat waves and dust devils leaped together in a hellish turmoil above its surface.

Tim again adventured toward the rocks, then veered off imperceptibly in the direction of the trees. He studied the ground, now and then looking up to examine the vacant hillsides. Perspiration was rolling like a cold bath under his shirt.

Just this side of the trees were a number of small shrubs in which one could find cover. Tim reached their outskirts.

Suddenly he dived behind a clump of sumac, then lifted himself and sprinted to the next cover. For an instant the rifleman held his fire. Then, as Tim rushed toward the trees, he began to shoot with hysterical rapidity.

Tim was almost to thick cover when the shot struck him; he spun round and tumbled, rolling over and over through the trees of the hillside. The rifleman jumped up better to see the effect of his hit. Tim, deep in cover now, his shoulder numb with bullet crease, crouched behind a pine and stared back.

Sven blundered out into the clear and came down the slope in long, lumbering strides. There was a white patch on him that would be a bandage.

Tim began to shake. He screamed and sprang into full view, sprinting down the hill and through the trees. The Winchester yapped excitedly behind him. Bark and branches showered him.

Tim emerged from the other side of the woods to plunge further. There was nothing between him and the desert now but odd blue gray boulders. Now and then the rifle behind him sounded as he flung himself from cover to cover in his flight.

Then he began to hear shots from another angle. Lingering for an instant he looked up the mountain and saw Bonnet, seated on a rock as though in target practice, patiently waiting for his game to come again into view. Tim now had to flee directly toward the alkali waste.

Below and before him a canyon mouth gaped into the blast furnace of the desert, weirdly shadowed in the slanting sunlight. Wind devils played and reeled, and the heat was like a magnet sucking moisture from the body.

Tim, stumbling and footsore, left the canyon and issued into the wind-torn flats, sinking to his ankles in the acrid dust.

The heat which was contained in the powdery alkali was incredible. He felt as though his stumbling legs were being cooked in ovens. Snowshoes alone would have made this white substance passable. The thought of them and the thought of the contrast of temperature was such that Tim looked instinctively to his right to the far-off range, across this waste, where winter's snow still lingered.

His startled glance stayed fixed in that direction for a minute. Tim veered, his objective hidden now and then by sighing dust devils which seemed to grow in number. There was something lying out there in the desert.

There was very little left of the man, despite the fact that he had been there only a few weeks. He was mummified, for no wolf had adventured here to feed. His burro was lying dead beside him, its legs stretched out stiffly, its fur white with the salts of the alkali.

The man was lying on his side, eyes open, skin so much parchment. Tim stepped beyond him and saw a bullet hole through the back of his head.

This then was one of Bonnet's companions. The body was partially sunken into the alkali and Tim yanked it out, scrabbled beneath it in a wild search for a weapon. There was nothing there but the man's worn clothes and the tattered shoes on his feet.

Tim crouched and looked back to the canyons which led up to the cool lush heights of Desperation Peak. He could see something moving now, eight hundred yards above and beyond the canyon's mouth. A feverish prayer sprang to his lips and he glanced beseechingly at the sky. He gripped his knife and sought to posture the burro in such a way that it might act as a shield. Whenever he moved the mummy, the sharp dust bit into his eyes and his nostrils, and the alkali salt settled over him and caked his hands and his face and his clothes.

Then, for the first time, he noticed how long the shadows were. He glanced toward the sun and found, with a shock, that he could not see it. There was a sighing in the air. It was not like the sibilance of the wind in the pines, but more vicious, like the hiss of a poisonous snake. Then a dust devil was all about him, filling his mouth and eyes with the hot acridness of alkali.

His lungs, already inflamed with running, began to shrivel within him. Over him, remorselessly played the gigantic column of dust, scorching him and suffocating him. It lessened and whipped back. Clearing his eyes for an instant as it receded, Tim had seen that the entire area about him was alive with these freakish whirlwinds. They filled the air with a fog which made sight impossible. He was smothered again then; choking darkness drifted down around him.

CHAPTER FOUR

FOR the better part of the night Bonnet and Sven ranged the flat, adventuring out upon it as far as a mile; then Bonnet returned to a spur of Desperation Peak immediately below their camp, to await Sven who still searched. At dawn Sven found Bonnet sleeping comfortably. Sven shook his shoulder.

"Coom up now, Mr. Bonnet. He vas dead, Aye think."

Bonnet sat up and rubbed his eyes; he replaced his hat, smoothed out his corduroy, blew a speck of dust out of the muzzle of his rifle, and looked out across the expanse already scorching in the morning sun. A fresh dust devil was spinning, a small one. As the day progressed they would grow larger and larger until at sunset the contrary and buffeting winds would entirely populate this hell with them. It was a bleak and depressing sight.

Bonnet sighed.

"He coom to his finish," said Sven. "It vas impossible to cross him until November. Huh, Mr. Bonnet?"

"Too bad," said Bonnet. "Sven, I feel like the buzzard denied of his prey, the jackal robbed of his carcass, the wolf cheated of his kill. Ungrateful of him, isn't it?"

"Three, four days he coom up with much sport," said Sven, scowling at Bonnet.

31

"Ah yes, Sven. But the kill, man, the kill. We yelled 'tallyho' and then didn't bring him to bay. We have no brush to show. Regrettable."

"Vat you mean, Mr. Bonnet?"

"Fox hunting," said Bonnet. "First one to the kill gets the fox's tail."

"It vas like mine head," said Sven, heavily.

"Ah yes, just like your head, Sven. Quite so." Bonnet looked out across the alkali flats and then sighed again. "The hunting is all well and good, Sven. But what's a hunt unless you come in at the end? He had us after all."

"He vas dead. Aye am sure," said Sven.

"But the alkali got him, we didn't," said Bonnet. "That's the difference."

"So long as he vas dead," said Sven. "All dot Aye vas interested in vas de gold. Coom up, Mr. Bonnet. Aye am hongry."

Bonnet rose languidly, stretched, put his rifle across his wrist and put his hands in his pockets. He sauntered up the slope after Sven, toward a greener elevation. Now and then Bonnet would look backward at the alkali flats which had cheated him. At last he resigned himself to it and grudgingly assigned to the desert its dead.

Sven quickened his pace as the music of the creek came to him. He trotted down into the bottom, crashed through some alder and floundered up to his knees in the stream. He bent and ducked himself, head and shoulders, into the reviving water. He came up and instantly grabbed at his gun.

32

Mr. Bonnet's howl of anger still echoed in the ravine. Sven looked every place for the source of annoyance, then stared at his master.

Bonnet was tearing through the rubble of his camp, throwing buckskin sacks left and right. Sven struggled up the slippery bank from the sluice and looked stupidly on.

"Do something!" Bonnet screamed at him. "Do something, you condemned fool! It's gone! It's gone, I tell you! Gone! Gone! Gone!" And Bonnet tore again at the empty buckskin sacks.

Sven walked to the shallow cache where the gold had lain in the forty sacks. It was empty. Bleak bewilderment came over him. He looked from the sluice to his master and back again.

Bonnet was running back and forth like a hound, rifle held so tight that his knuckles, like his face, were pasty gray. Every now and then he would stop and shout at Sven, "Do something!"

Bonnet's circles were growing wider and his actions wilder. He turned and threw his hat at Sven. "Circle out and pick up his track!" he shouted.

Sven picked up the two remaining canteens. "He vas took vater, yes."

Bonnet came back, quivering, and then halted, staring at a plain footprint in the damp bank. Beside it was the impression of Sven's huge sole. Mr. Bonnet pointed at it. Sven came up and looked at it thoughtfully.

"It vasn't him," said Sven. He scratched his head. "It vasn't me and it vasn't you and it vasn't him."

Bonnet's face was becoming dark. "It was Sims, you bungler. I leave you to do a thing and you botch it; you'd be dead if it weren't for me!"

Sven looked stupidly at the footprint. "But he vas hit over the ear with my fist. It vas a hard blow. Aye tell you. His skull vas cracked. He vas in the middle of the desert vithout vater!"

"It was Sims!" shouted Bonnet. "He followed us through and he's waited here, laughing at us. He just waited until we were gone long enough so he could take the gold!"

"Maybe it vas that Cormoree half-breed," said Sven.

"No! No! No!" said Bonnet, impatiently. "It wasn't Cormoree. I blew his brains out myself. I tell you it's that Sims. Spread out. Pick up his trail. It ought to be easy to follow him while he's carrying all that gold."

Sven looked at the track. "It vasn't the young one. His heel tore off. Yah, it must be Sims. Aye vas hitting a veak blow; forgive me, Mr. Bonnet."

But Bonnet wasn't paying any attention to Sven. A yip of elation came from him. He had moved down the ravine. Sven lumbered down to where Bonnet was and found him bending over a track. There were the footprints again across a wet place; beside them, deeply sunken, were the hoof-marks of a jenny.

"Look," said Bonnet. "It's like I tell you. He got back to the other side after you hit him. And he came on through with a burro. He's been waiting here, watching us while we wasted our time hunting that young fool of a miner. Sims actually made it back despite the desert all around here; he brought a burro!"

34

"Yah," said Sven. "The burro vas carrying a heavy load."

"He was carrying two hundred thousand dollars' worth of gold," said Bonnet. "Come along. Be quick now. He can't be very far ahead. If he tried to head back across the sink, we may catch up to him. He won't go fast through that soft alkali. Not with a cargo like that burro's carrying. Oh, we'll get you, Mr. Sims! Fill up the canteens!"

Sven rushed back and dipped the two remaining canteens in the stream, capped them and looked up to find that Bonnet was already well down the mountain. Sven lumbered after him.

From rise to rise, bending his eyes always toward the desert, blazing now under the morning sun, Bonnet made his excited way. He cut off all the angles of the trail which would have been made necessary by the zigzagging of a burro down a steep grade. Now and then he and Sven would lose the spoor entirely, only to pick it up further on.

They were content to catch it in spots because the course obviously tended toward the desert, and they knew that the alkali dust would reveal much. Sims, they knew, would have to cross desert to get out of here and it didn't matter where he entered it. They would find the track.

At last they came to the place where the boulders thinned and the sinks began. Out there in that boiling hell lay certain death unless they were extremely careful of their water. This place could drink a man dry in six hours, squeeze him to death. It could suck out his juice and leave him a mummy in less than a day.

Sven, snuffling eagerly, found the place where the tracks led out. And with Bonnet close beside him, face muffled to the eyes with a scarf, Sven struck off into the alkali. The canteens banged together. Bonnet floundered through the powder, watching the spoor ahead, eyes lifting eagerly to find his game.

For three hours they traveled on the trail, conserving their water. Then, anxiety dying through the toil of walking, they rested for a moment.

"He can't be far," said Bonnet.

"Ve'll coom up with him," said Sven, "und then you vas get your kill. Huh, Mr. Bonnet?"

Bonnet grinned and reached for the canteen. It was curiously light in his hand and he stared at it. He pulled out the cork and excitedly uptilted it. A solitary drop came out.

Sven, in the sudden nausea of terror, uncorked the other canteen. It was empty as well. They stood up. Bonnet looked out into the desert and then turned slowly to look back at Desperation Peak, three hours of fast travel behind them—*twelve miles*!

But they couldn't travel as fast on the return, and they had not drunk on the way out. The hottest, most aching part of the day remained. The desert sun and the alkali were drinking heavily from Bonnet's body, till the extraction of water was a physical sensation. He looked at the empty canteen in his hand and then turned it up to examine it.

It did not matter now, nothing mattered now, but there was a small hole made by the point of a knife in the canteen's bottom from which the water had drip, drip, dripped, to evaporate before it ever struck the ground.

Bonnet stared at Desperation Peak. Sven was already beginning to lumber back toward the first spur of the distant mountain. It was so deceptively near, the green meadows, the green trees, so cool and inviting. Sven stumbled on, faster now, floundering, blowing hard as he lumbered through the alkali, surging back in animal desperation for a life which his mind knew was already forfeited.

Bonnet looked at the track which led out into the alkali wastes, fixed his spyglass to his eye. The hot metal of the rim burned him but he gazed thoughtfully. The track led on for another half a mile and then curved slowly to the right to head back toward Desperation Peak. It passed within five hundred yards of the outgoing trail, angling off and getting wider. Bonnet crossed the bow and found the returning spoor. He was reeling already from thirst.

He went outward along it a little way, for there was no jenny here—only a man and a man walking light. This puzzled him and he thought perhaps he might find the gold. But ten minutes later he knew that even this satisfaction was to be denied him.

Beside the trail, indifferently covered with alkali dust, were the two front legs of a mummified burro. They had been sawed off at the knees with a knife. There were also two tattered old boots with peculiar red tops. He recognized them instantly as belonging to the half-breed Cormoree, whom he had murdered.

Bonnet smiled wanly as he looked at these "tracking irons." "What a fool I am," he thought to himself. One of these hoofs even had a nick in it, a flaw which, if his greed had not blinded him, would easily have disclosed that two hoofs, not four, had been used.

He had been fooled; while they had searched in the wastes, the trap had been laid for them last night. The hunters had been trapped by the fox. The young miner would be back there lying beside a cool stream by now.

Bonnet turned and looked back at Desperation Peak. The dust devils were gathering with the approaching noontide. The exhaustion of moisture from him was such as to make him faint. It was easily a hundred and forty degrees here, and death would not be too pleasant.

Sven was merely a speck, stumbling more often now, picking himself up to rush on, a hopeless, degrading figure in the near distance. The major portion of his journey was yet to be traveled. He would obviously never make it.

Bonnet breathed a contemptuous, "Animal." He took out his Colt. The metal was hot to his touch. In a moment he would not mind that; he placed the muzzle to his temple and pulled the trigger.

The shot ranged faintly across the alkali wasteland and was swallowed up in the sing of the whirling dust devils.

In the distance, Sven turned, wiped a shaking hand across his cracked lips, and looked back. His small eyes picked out the huddled dot. He convulsively took two steps toward it before he understood. Sven staggered and then, face hidden in his hands, sank down hopelessly to wait.

Tim Beckdolt came back from the spur from which he had been watching. He walked wearily up the gully toward his placer, came to the spot where the water sank away. He bathed his face and went on. Just before dusk he arrived at his diggings. He sat down, tiredly.

He emptied the remainder of the water from his canteens on the ground and put them aside to sweeten. Methodically he cut long strips from the haunch of venison which Sven had killed and left to hang on a pine tree. He restrained an impulse to devour it raw and built a fire to roast it.

Carefully, daintily, he cut the meat into small strips. He bit into it and felt the nourishment soaking into his body. He kept himself from eating too much, made himself put the meal away half finished.

He stood up and rubbed his aching shoulder, where the bullet had creased him, turned to look out across the sunset where the dust devils ranged on the alkali flats. They had been so sure of themselves; he had known they would be. When darkness had come he had realized, in hunger's brilliant thinking, that they were sure.

While they had hunted for him on the flats he had put on the dead man's shoes and cut off the burro's front legs. He had come in for the canteens which he would need, had hidden the gold and punctured the canteens that he had left. Then he had laid his trap and it had worked. They had been so greedy and so sure—so eager to follow the false trail.

He straightened and squared his shoulders. It was not pleasant to kill men so, with punctured canteens and thirst on the maddening alkali flats. Tim was too young to do it without a shudder, even though he had to, to save his own life.

He went down to the creek, picked up the shovel, *his* shovel, and began to scoop away the mud from under the sluices and load it into the riffles. Presently, as the discolored water ran clear, gold began to gleam in the rocks beneath the sluice where he had dumped it the night before.

On the bank he ranged up the sacks. From the mud he began to pull up shovels of the pure gold and dump them for cleaning in the sluice. They'd wanted it so hard, and here it was. But they were dead now, dead and mummies out there in the alkali. He shuddered again and addressed himself to his work.

He shoveled on and on, and as he shoveled, he at length began to whistle. A blue jay mocked him and a squirrel chattered in the pine tree over his head. The woods were sweet and the water sang an accompaniment.

As he whistled he began to dream of what his stepfather would have to say now.

It was very quiet and very still as the sunset played its splendid hues on the slopes of the sleeping mountain.

JOHNNY, THE TOWN TAMER

JOHNNY, THE TOWN TAMER

THE toughest town on the railroad was Thorpeville. It had been named for a surveyor who had been jumped by Apaches here in '71 and obliterated, and whose grave was now no less so on a knoll amongst the tin cans south of the tracks.

At the moment in history when Johnny tackled Thorpeville, that squalid cluster of shacks and loading pens was the current end of the Texas trail, whence came tens of thousands of heads of beef to be shipped to Kansas City and tens of dozens of Texas punchers to be bilked, cheated, knocked out, poisoned, shot and mayhemed.

Just now Thorpeville sat in the middle of a sea of prairie mud, the spring rains being late here, and waited for the first of the long, bawling herds which would come and make the citizenry, namely George Bart, solvent once more. Cattle buyers waited in boredom around the New York House, gamblers and their cohorts shuffled cards disconsolately, dance halls had the desolate and deceptive air of churches.

George Bart was all ready for the brisk trade which would last the next many months. As sole agent for more things than any respectable man would want, Bart had caused his warehouse—the only warehouse—to be full of cases and bottles which gurgled, barrels which sloshed and kegs which purled, as well as more mundane articles such as canned corn, pineapple, peaches, tomatoes and peas, as well as bulging sacks of dried beans and casks of brined beef. George was what might have been called a monopolist; he ran the New York House, the New York Bar, the New York Restaurant and the Gilded Cage Dance Hall. He wholesaled anything he might have left over to the few smaller establishments and kept them from growing by the simple arithmetic of canceling out whatever owner seemed to challenge the main trade.

A man of Bart's temperament and philosophy (which was that them as grabs gits) takes very unkindly to competition in any field. Therefore, he courted the best-looking girl, drove the best gig, wore the most expensive boots and drank the most whiskey of anyone in town. His dislike of competition went so far as to hire only those marshals who could not shoot as good as George. Not, of course, that George did much shooting; there were several indefinite-eyed gents around the New York House who generally attended to the more sordid business details of the Bart empire.

The railroad had been here for a long time, it had not gone any further because of certain Bartlike proceedings back in Wall Street. So Bart was a railhead and Thorpeville, unless drivers wanted to trail another two hundred and fifty miles, was the logical and inevitable destination of the Texas herds.

George ran his kingdom and was entirely satisfied with it. Texans had to come into it and were just as intensely dissatisfied. But there was nothing they could do, they had to sell their cattle, and two hundred and fifty miles in the drag is a long, long ways to ride.

This morning the prairie looked drier, a number of crocuses were out, as well as shooting stars, and a meadowlark was trying to bust his throat over behind the graveyard. The citizenry did not expect a herd today or for many days, a river still being in flood to the south, and they did not at first recognize the appearance of a lone Texan as the symbol that their season of rapine and robbery had begun.

Johnny Austin Darryl, somewhat better known as Sudden Johnny, owner of the Double G down Matagordas way, was thin and muddy in his saddle. But his gun was not muddy; he had stopped outside town and cleaned that weapon with great care and love, crooning the while in an off-key tenor that there would be blood on the barroom floor that night.

His herd was ten days' drive behind him because of a swollen river and because they'd need rail cars on arrival in Thorpeville. But the ordering of said cars was not the reason Sudden Johnny had come north, nor why he had ridden in advance. There were plenty of things on the Double G to demand the owner's attention and he had five men, any one of whom would have made an entirely competent trail boss. Well, not entirely competent; Greg Matson had brought the herd last year, which was why Sudden Johnny was here.

He rode to the middle of the main and only street and looked at the imposing falsity of the New York House, the New York Bar and the New York Restaurant, all of which bore the legend that Geo. Bart was sole owner and proprietor.

"Son," said Johnny to a man about eighty years old sitting on a porch, "could you kindly direct me to the person of this here George Bart?"

45

"Son!" cried the oldster. "Look here—"

"Can it, pop," said George Bart. He had a nose for business and anybody with a squint could read Texas on Sudden Johnny. "Howdy, cowboy. Git down and come in."

Sudden Johnny looked over his prey. George Bart was about six-six. He carried a sawed-off Lefevre shotgun in a holster, wore a big diamond in his Windsor tie, and he had a look on his face which might have fooled a foolish fly but not another tarantula. "You Bart?"

"I'm Bart."

Sudden Johnny threw his reins to the oldster and roweled up to the porch of the New York House.

Bart read what he could of the mount's brand through the mud, then looked at Johnny. Some indefinable warning went through the monopolist, a faculty he had which accounted for his living so long. "Come in and have a drink," said Bart.

Johnny was looking up and down the street and sizing the town; this man probably had hired guns and friends behind every counter. He looked back at Bart. Northerners had funny ideas about shooting, even skunks, for Johnny, although definitely a gentleman living by a strict code, was not fool enough to exercise much etiquette on Bart.

This, then, was what Greg Matson had faced. He had received payment for two thousand longhorns, had distributed spending money to his men and shortly afterward awakened in the road, slug-happy and flat broke. The Double G had had to creep mighty easy through the past winter without that cash. Greg recalled being invited into a game in a back room and no more; somebody in Thorpeville owed Sudden Johnny fifteen thousand dollars and that somebody was probably George Bart.

"Your outfit comin'?" said Bart.

"Yuh. The river's up. Don't you ever get spring up here?"

"It'll go back in a few days," said Bart. "Come ahead to order cars?"

"Yeh. Where's the agent?"

"Over in that shack. When you get through come back and have a drink, you must be pretty thirsty."

"I'm thirsty all right," said Sudden Johnny. "Hungry, too." He went down the steps and across the street to the indicated shack.

When he came out he found that they had stabled his horse for him; he went into the New York Bar and found Bart.

"Give him the best," Bart told the bartender.

Johnny poured a careful glass. He was known somewhat as a drinking man down Matagordas. It was said he could hold more liquor than anybody in that end of Texas, but this of course was a considerable exaggeration for Johnny almost never got drunk.

He had three to start his circulation going and then insisted on paying for them. "No, no. Hell, no," said Bart. "Glad to have you come here, don't worry none."

Johnny took out a poke. "Well, maybe you wouldn't accept gold dust anyway. It's all the hard money I got."

"Gold dust?" said Bart, looking at the long poke. "Where'd that come from? I ain't never seen any from yore part of the country."

"Ain't," said Johnny. "It's from Mexico. We shipped down a lot of stuff by boat and they paid us in this stuff. Yucatán, most likely. People generally will take it, though, it's worth about seventeen dollars a ounce."

Bart looked at the bright flakes and his eyes heated a trifle. "Let's see some closer."

Johnny put a dab of the stuff in the outstretched palm and Bart picked it over, glancing now and then at the tall poke of it. "You must have plenty in that sack. How much, you think?"

"Five, six thousand, that's all," said Johnny.

Bart shivered and put the subject aside for the moment with some effort. It was an obvious strain.

"Wouldn't have been able to have made my drive if the Mexes hadn't paid out," said Johnny. "Come through just in time. Well, here's mud in your eye." He drank again with a quick jerk of his wrist and put the poke back, evidently forgetting the tiny amount he had given Bart.

"Here, cowboy," said Bart. "I shore don't want to be considered dishonest. I invited you to drink up and I meant it, this here is your gold."

"Oh, so it is," said Johnny, taking it back into the poke which he again put away.

Johnny was looking the place over. When you are getting ready to tear things apart, board by board, it's a good thing to get a careful idea of how they go together.

This was one big room with a bar and tables in it with windows on the opposite wall from the bar. A big double door at the back was open to daylight and beyond it lay what seemed to be Bart's warehouse. Two slanted doors went down a flight of steps. This was a sod house below-ground level, cool and comfortable, probably the original Thorpeville complete. A cook was struggling up the steps with a box of sardines under one arm and a keg of wine under the other. When he reached the top he shut the doors and snapped a padlock in place.

Johnny saw that the left rear of this barroom gave into a couple of small anterooms. A door opened here into the lobby of the New York House. He nodded to himself, shifted his gun belt and felt of his stubbly jaw. "Reckon," he said, "I'll shave me up a trifle. I ain't ridin' back, too blamed comfortable here."

"Sure. We'll have her fixed right up for you," said Bart. "Ain't a bedbug in the place. Joe! Show Mr.— You didn't say yore name."

"They call me Johnny."

"Joe, show Mr. Johnny at a room and let the Chinese lug him a bath." He smiled upon Johnny. "When you come down, mebbe we can have a little excitement like a game of cards. It shore is dull hereabouts."

"Suits me," said Johnny, "but all I got is gold dust."

"Reckon I won't quibble none about that, seein' you probably got two–three thousand cattle in a trail herd down here as well. Pete already took in your war sack when he cared for your hoss."

"Much obliged," said Johnny.

It was afternoon when he came down. He had had a sleep and grub and he felt up to his game. He was burnished from the labors of the Chinese and bright in a calico shirt. Johnny had his campaign pretty well mapped, he'd spent a long time mapping it. The only time he'd ever go sudden was when action began, which befitted a grandnephew of Beauregard.

George Bart had fixed up a back room very tastefully with a large array of bottles on a sideboard, a quantity of edibles and a table on which lay a new deck of cards and around which sat, waiting very patiently, men who would have stayed there day and night for a week if Bart had told them to.

Johnny walked in and found a very smiling and hospitable George. "Well, we was hoping you'd be down, Mr. Johnny. A few boys like yourself drifted in and we was about to have a game. Have something to drink first?"

They drank, then George pulled back a chair. Johnny was expected to get into that chair but it had its back to the door and was flanked too closely. Johnny took another which suited him better and Bart less.

Johnny picked up the cards, broke their seal and shuffled them. He gave a quick look around the table and saw nothing but hard, gaunt faces about as full of expression as a sidewinder's. Johnny grinned at them companionably.

The door of the outer saloon opened and a man came in, a big man even as Texans go. He wore mainly buckskin, about three or four deer's worth of it, stained with mud and grease. He had a beard, a black beard, thick enough to be bulletproof. If, from where he sat, Sudden Johnny shot this newcomer any glance, none noticed, so intent were they on getting their first cards.

Johnny had delayed. Spanish Mike McCarty was something

more than Johnny's top rider, he was also Johnny's friend. Johnny's height had slenderness and his movements had grace, but Mike's chief attribute was a mountainous strength which sometimes fell on men and cured them of things, including living.

Spanish Mike combed some of the mud out of his beard, ordered a beer mug of whiskey, scooped up one handful of pretzels—one pound—from the free lunch and composed himself at the bar. He too had paused on the edge of town but not to clean his gun. He had halted to separate his arrival from Johnny's by several unsuspicious hours and had profited by a nice relaxing snooze in the mud. Mike looked over the premises, looked out through the back door, sighed in pure delight and relaxed to watch the game.

Sudden Johnny dealt to a somewhat dumbfounded crowd. He had been clumsy enough when he shuffled the cards but somehow these cards weren't the cards which had been carefully rewrapped and placed in the center of the table. They were honest cards and there were glowers of wonder at George Bart at this supposed oversight. When the bartender served from the sideboard he caught a terrible pain in his shins—not serious, for his grimace vanished instantly as he moved away from Bart.

"I plumb forgot about money," said Johnny. "This poke is all I brought and this kind of makes it look like I'm playin' on credit." He hitched at the poke in his back pocket.

"Now don't you fret about money," said George Bart. "I'm shore you can cover if you lose. Besides, there's yore trail herd."

"So there is," said Johnny and picked up his hand.

They played for a round before Johnny discovered abruptly that he was using a new deck. He found he was using it because it didn't have creases on the aces where he had put them. He lost promptly, stud being a quick game, but one deal later, being Johnny's, found them playing with another new deck.

Bart's abrupt shift from returned confidence to new alarm registered the shift. Johnny did not win very much but the deck stayed in for five deals until the bartender accidentally placed his tray on the momentarily idle cards.

Johnny was playing with Bart's deck once more.

The lose was going to him then, steadily, and his chips dwindled, somebody lighted a kerosene lantern over the table and the shadows of it made the faces around that board appear longer and gaunter.

The whiskey kept coming and Johnny's chips kept going down. At last he gave Mike a private wink. Mike instantly drained off the remainder of his whiskey, crammed down the rest of his free lunch and stood a little straighter at the bar, twenty feet away.

"Reckon," said Johnny, "I'll have to cash in for tonight, boys, it's been a long day."

"Well, I hate to break up a good game," said Bart.

"Tell you what," said Johnny, "I'll cut you double or quits."

"Well, now, Mr. Johnny, I couldn't do that. I reckon the best thing is just cash you in."

Johnny shrugged. He reached back for the poke and then

managed to look most terribly astonished and mad. It was gone! The bartender!

"My gold!" said Johnny. "I had it when I sat down here. I guess I'll—"

"Well, now, Mr. Johnny, don't let that worry you. Seein' that them blue chips was worth exactly one thousand apiece. I can always take a trail herd."

"One thousand!" said Johnny.

"Why, you didn't ask and I thought—"

Johnny smiled. He pulled three packs of cards out of his lap and dropped them on the board. "I reckon, then, you'd maybe like to explain somethin' else you forgot to mention, George. These here cards you use just plain read too easy—"

"You accusin' me of card cheatin'?" bellowed George.

"Why, no," said Sudden Johnny. "I meant to call you a dirty, lyin' card cheat!"

With a crash the kerosene light went out. The fragments and bits of flame splattered, Spanish Mike fired three more shots and put the main barroom in darkness.

The table came up like a battering ram and slammed George into the wall. Johnny's gun blazed and Bart's man Tolliver curled into himself with a groan, three guns racketed at the spot where Johnny had been but Johnny wasn't there.

"Yeeeow!" he yelled to Spanish Mike.

"Yowheee!" screamed Spanish Mike.

"They're out the back!" bawled Bart and hurriedly thundered after them.

Sudden Johnny, like all good grandnephews of Beauregard,

had his second line to fall back upon when his first one buckled; he might not have made it with the cards and he might have lost his poke, but there was no indecision now. He and Mike went at the warehouse flaps in a dive and Mike's big fist wrenched off the lock.

They plummeted down the steps and whirled to slam the doors back upon them. An instant later a body hit wood outside and somebody bawled for them to come out. Johnny shot cunningly by feel and there was a *yowp* of anguish immediately after.

By the flash of the shot, Mike found the inner bar and placed it across. The doors strained up and Johnny fired again. Their assailants shot a dozen times into the door and tried to prize it open at a distance, using rails.

Mike grunted with busyness; he was loading up the stairs with assorted crates and barrels, and so great was his strength and so rapidly did he work that the next shots fired from outside went into wood and tin.

This big below-ground warehouse had been built long ago and it had been built well. It had served as defense against Indians and cyclones and its thick sod walls were glued together by grass roots and many rains. Johnny inspected loopholes, found one which commanded the back of the New York Bar and gave them six shots as fast as he could fan. That instantly ended the attack.

Mike mopped his brow. "Well, Johnny, here we be. And here it appears we are goin' to stay for some time to come. If you got no great objections, that keg I seen by yore gun flashes must contain high wine."

Johnny inspected loopholes, found one which commanded the back of the New York Bar and gave them six shots as fast as he could fan. That instantly ended the attack.

They found it, they broached it. Big Spanish Mike lay down on his back, held up the keg like it was a bottle and had himself a good, long drink—a half gallon.

"Thin stuff," he belched. "Never much cared for wine." He put it down and went feeling through the interior over a fortune in liquors and food. A loud pop startled him. "What's that?"

"That," said Sudden Johnny, "is champagne."

Spanish Mike listened to the gurgle with a grin.

By midnight, George Bart had snarled and sweated himself into a fine fury. They had pried the door half off before they discovered that the passage was blocked beyond their ability to open it from the outside, and they had lost in wounded three men, all of whom damned George heartily with what breath they could muster.

"Condemned Texicans!" snarled Tolliver, gray with a chip gone off a rib. "I tole you you ought to think twicet afore ringin' that gent 'round."

"You never said no such thing," said Dutch stolidly. "All you said was you wanted a hundred bucks instead of fifty."

"Do you mean to tell me," said Bart to his assembled five, "that you won't charge that door again?"

"You know danged well we won't!" gritted Tolliver. "Wait for mornin', I says, then blow 'em sky-wide and handsome with blastin' powder."

They looked on this with favor and arranging a watch amongst them, excluding Tolliver, the one wounded man who was still with them, they retired from the field for the night.

56

In the morning the meadowlarks were singing brightly, the prairie was blooming but very, very wet, and a freighter came in from Hunter for supplies.

His storekeeper routed George Bart from a nightmare. "Freighter down there with a big order. I can't fill half of it from the shelves."

"Get it from the warehouse!" growled George from his untidy lair. Then he suddenly remembered. He hastily got on his clothes and went down to see the store.

"I can't wait, Mr. Bart," said the freighter. "We was held up plenty by the rains and we're nigh outa grub. I need more than Lem here can give me but if that's all, why it's the best I can do. I got to git back. Men's hungry."

Bart looked at the stripped shelves and then at the pile of money. The freighter was about to leave. "Wait," said George. "We've had—well, a little accident. But I think maybe I can get something up by two o'clock if you'll just wait around."

The freighter was doubtful and George Bart clinched it by striding over to the depot where he found the agent just coming to work. "Henry," said Bart, "get me a message through to Sioux. I need some things on—"

"Hello, Mr. Bart," said Henry with a dash of malice. "I hear you got a couple prisoners locked up in yore storehouse."

Bart glared. "Get me a message through to Sioux, they'll bring it in on the two o'clock for me."

"Mr. Bart," said Henry, "I sure hate to disappoint you but there's a bridge out between here and there and she ain't likely to be fixed for weeks."

"A washout! I didn't know the rain was that bad."

"It wasn't," said Henry. "It just so happens that that bridge seems to have blown out. Why, I ain't got the faintest notion; it'll be back in come first part of next month."

"Blown out!" cried Bart. "Look here, Henry—wait a minute. When did that happen?"

"Seems like night before last. They was a feller in here yesterday to give to me the word and I sent it on through."

"A limber gent with brown eyes? A Texican?"

"Yep, reckon so. He seen it on his ride in. Can't say whar he come from. But there's no gettin' across the river without that bridge. Don't seem hardly important, though. There ain't no herds here yet and we'll be able to ship 'em all when they do come. I sent word through to Sioux and that, not this, is the end of the line. Means a sort of vacation—"

Bart had already left. He told the freighter angrily that he couldn't give any more supplies and watched the man drive away. He went to the back of the New York Bar and stood looking at the sod warehouse.

Dutch was on guard. "Ain't stirred, Mr. Bart," he said.

"Go on over there and tell them to come out or we'll blow 'em out!" said George.

A shot made a neat hole just above Bart's head and he hurriedly skittered back; it upset him. A splinter had nicked his ear and he looked thoughtfully at the blood, swearing the while but subdued. "I'll find a way," he muttered. After breakfast, George felt better in that his breakfast always went down along with a mug of brandy and water. He was almost cheerful when he came into the store. "Let's have a keg of

Giant and a lot of fuse," he said. "It won't take much to blow in a wall."

The storekeeper stood fixed.

"Well?" shouted Bart. "Where is it?"

"I sold it!" said Lem. "That freighter wanted two kegs and all the rest is in the back end of the warehouse."

Bart whirled and bumped into Dutch. "Saddle up and ride after that freighter!" he ordered. "Bring back a keg of Giant powder, and don't fail!"

Dutch ran out and Tolliver limped up, hand to his punctured ribs. "I think they're drunk in there, boss. I heard the dangedest yowls comin' out of there. Thought somebody was mortal hurt until I heerd the words to the 'Streets of Laredo.' They're drinkin' up the entire stock!"

"That," said Bart, "would take a powerful lot of drinkin'. They ain't got long for it noways. Dutch—"

Dutch was coming back, white-faced and racing. "Boss! The stableman is over there all tied up and there ain't a single condemned hoss in the hull danged town!"

They hurried to confirm it and found the Star Barn entirely empty except for the stableman who, gagged all night, wanted to cuss somebody good and proper and didn't care just who.

Bart finally cut through the fanfare. "Who did it?"

"I didn't see good. A big man in greasy buckskin and a beard. He come in and said he wanted to wash down his own hoss and then by jimminies, the skunk whopped me. I come to in an empty stable and not a one of you rannies come near me the hull danged night! I—"

Bart stared at the end of the sod warehouse he could see from here. The morning sun was bright, the meadowlarks were singing and the prairie was steaming dry. But there was no loveliness in the view to him. He suddenly threw down his hat and jumped on it.

> . . . cowpuncher lay dyin'
> Cowpuncher lay dyin'
> As cold as the clay . . .

It came faintly but even at this distance there were hiccoughs in it.

As the days followed, freighters came and riders came. The food swiftly diminished in Thorpeville and after the fifth day not even a jackrabbit could be shot a decent walk from the place. As long as the river to the south remained swollen, no beef would come in and very soon the two hundred population of the community were notching up their belts tighter and taking speculative looks at one another.

The effort to send a wire for help met with failure; there was too much water to the east and no wagon could cross here for a while. Repairs were being made on the bridge but this was also slow and difficult due to the floods.

Then it began to rain again and made matters much worse. Half a dozen at a time began to walk out of Thorpeville, down along the tracks, knowing they could raft or swim the break in the rails and maybe catch a handcar ride to Sioux, a hundred miles down the tracks. A telegram Henry got said that a train was there making repairs and would transport

GET 4 FREE BOOKS!

You can have the titles in the Stories from the Golden Age delivered to your door by signing up for the book club. Start today, and we'll send you **4 FREE BOOKS** (worth $39.80) as your reward.

〈◦〉

The collection includes 80 volumes (book or audio) by master storyteller L. Ron Hubbard in the genres of science fiction, fantasy, mystery, adventure and western, originally penned for the pulp magazines of the 1930s and '40s.

〈◦〉

YES! ☑

Sign me up for the Stories from the Golden Age Book Club and send me my first book for $9.95 with my **4 FREE BOOKS** (FREE shipping). I will pay only $9.95 each month for the subsequent titles in the series. Shipping is FREE and I can cancel any time I want to.

First Name _____ Middle Name _____ Last Name _____

Address _____

City _____ State _____ ZIP _____

Telephone _____ E-mail _____

Credit/Debit Card #: _____

Card ID# (last 3 or 4 digits): _____ Exp Date: _____ / _____

Date (month/day/year) _____ / _____ / _____

Signature: _____

Comments: _____

Thank you!

To sign up online, go to: **www.GoldenAgeStories.com**

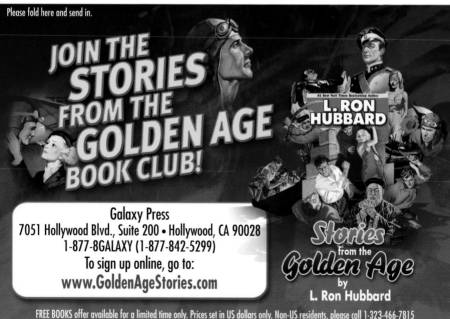

from there. It was only sixty miles. Why wait? The population began to walk.

The constant guard of the sod house occasionally sought to surprise the alertness of its inmates. Various expedients were tried, such as shooting with rifles through the slots from long range, pushing burning boxes up against the doors, promises of money in return for a parley, two outright charges and three sneak attacks at night.

All efforts failed. No matter how many songs came out of that warehouse to badger and irritate the guards, a foray was met with shots. George Bart was getting exactly noplace. It had been going on for two and a half weeks when George, one morning, found he had a population of exactly fifteen. Nine of these were too old to walk, four of them were his gunmen, one was his bartender (who was thought to have a secret store, he stayed so fat) and the remaining one was Bart himself. There was a little food left. Somebody had shot a locoed horse out on the prairie and they could live if they didn't object to horse meat.

The prairie was drying again. The river to the south was reported down by an oldster who had gone out and shot himself a private deer. George Bart felt that if he could just hold on until a train could come through he would bring up troops.

Henry, the telegraph operator, had long since taken his own handcar down to the bridge and left it there as thoroughly as he had left his resignation of office on his desk. George Bart could not read the clicks and clacks of the instrument; he could only stand on the platform, listen at the window, and hope that the occasional sputters meant relief had already started.

It was in this condition that Greg Matson and four Texicans found Thorpeville. They had forded with their cattle and they held them now on the prairie about a mile from the loading pens, the first herd through of the season.

They were promptly approached, as they started to ride in, leaving two of their number to ride guard, by George Bart. "I want to buy cattle!" said Bart.

Greg Matson had a beard now and its stiff bristles hid him from recognition. "We got cattle. Thirty dollars a head, two thousand head. Prime beef, all fed up to weigh south of the cro—"

"I don't want a herd!" cried Bart. "I want a dozen steers!"

Greg sat his horse thoughtfully. "Now, ain't that unfortunate, I only sell in two-thousand-head lots today."

Bart kept his temper. He was hungry. He usually ate a lot. "All right. I'll buy the herd. Come on up to my office and I'll give you the fair price."

This looked like an easy victory. Greg and two men rode forward watchfully, keeping pace with the men on foot and finally came to the New York House. The Texicans followed inside, very alert.

George opened his safe and got out a stack of bills. He kept a lot of money on hand to buy up cattle buyers who had lost too much and he brought out a thick sheaf of bills.

Under the bills lay a Derringer; ranged round the Texicans were four men.

His office window was very grimy and broken in one place but he had eyes only for the Texicans before him. He started to swing, Derringer cocked. "Look out!" yelled Sudden Johnny at the window.

Bart tried to swing back and shoot. Dutch, diving for cover, upset him and the Derringer whammed into the safe door, both barrels.

A chair and then Johnny came through the window. A knife flashed and Spanish Mike finished Dutch, square in the doorway, blocking all exit.

The noise in the room was loud and painful and long, and then from the din of smoke and swearing came Sudden Johnny—dragging George Bart by the collar. They reached the street and George pitched into the mud.

Johnny let him get up and knocked him squarely down again. George rose a second time and went down a second time. He tottered to his feet a third and went suddenly backwards into a water trough where, except for the mercy of his opponent, he most certainly would have drowned.

Sudden Johnny brought him back to the walk and dumped him down much like a man dumps a sack of spuds. His four Texicans came out, bringing what was left of Bart's crew.

It was a very quiet town. A very quiet, deserted town.

It is rumored that George Bart paid back fifteen thousand that day as well as a poke of brass filings found in his possession. It is also rumored that George Bart sold his town, some say for ten thousand, others for eight.

The truth of the matter is, as Spanish Mike afterward told while deeply drunk, George presented the whole place to Sudden Johnny when he saw the state of that warehouse; presented it, and took the first train out for points unknown.

The state of the warehouse, gloated Spanish Mike, was at once a wonderful and dreadful thing to see.

STRANGER IN TOWN

STRANGER IN TOWN

THE stranger came riding through the hot white dust, and Zeke Tomlin stared.

It was a broiling afternoon in Dry Creek and few were abroad. Even the dogs failed to move out of the stranger's path, but lay sluggish in their hollows of sand and suffered their fleas to bite. A drunken Indian was weaving an erratic course between the 'dobe houses of the single street, stopping now and then to shake a bottle at an imaginary foe. The stranger came abreast of the Indian and the redman straightened, looked up and sobered a little.

Hunger was on the stranger's face and guns, like a stamp. Man-hunger, with kill in his eyes.

Zeke Tomlin had been wiping the packing grease from a buffalo rifle. He looked at it and put it down. It was cool in the hardware store but there were no visitors. Zeke, the clerk, was alone behind the counter. A rack of guns backed him, each newly taken from its case. Zeke looked up at the stranger and felt sick and hot.

It was a long time back to Mesa. Nine months. It was a long time back to the hunted trail he had followed away from there. He had thought it was all done and forgotten. And here was Les Harmon, riding through the hot white dust, come to kill him.

It is a terrible thing to be hunted, Zeke knew that. He could see the faces of dead men now, between the storefront and the street. Les Harmon, the sheriff of Mesa, would shoot on sight and shoot to kill.

What would they think of Zeke Tomlin in Dry Creek then? He was respected. He could mend their saddles and stand up to their poker bluffs. He said "Howdy" to the marshal and voted in the elections. But he had only been there nine months. He was a stranger in town.

He was a stranger in town who had come riding one dusk on a wind-broken horse to fall from his saddle over by the Golden Horn. They'd given him water and they'd found him a job. He had stayed. He had never quite belonged, some of these men had known each other all their lives.

If Les Harmon told them the story, they'd be ashamed they'd known Zeke; they'd believe a lawman. Dry Creek's marshal, Tom Brennerman, would buy Les a drink and the man from Mesa would ride away. If Zeke yelled now, Harmon would tell what he knew. If he didn't yell, Harmon would kill him. If he killed Harmon—well, they hanged a man who killed the law, didn't they?

Zeke's throat was dry and hot. He looked across to see Les Harmon watering his horse in front of the Golden Horn. Harmon would flash his badge and ask for Zeke Tomlin. Then he'd come across the street—Zeke tried to swallow and found he couldn't.

There was no sense in running. Dry Creek was the only town in this large cattle basin, beyond that the desert was dry and wide and a horse left tracks. And then there was his leg. He had not done much riding after Les Harmon's .44 had taken him nine months and more ago.

He was caught. Time had kept the trail open, not closed it. Les Harmon had not given up.

Zeke tried to think of how he could have given his whereabouts away, but all Zeke could think about was the trail which had stayed open.

It had started innocently enough: a fight in a saloon where a bartender had tried to take all Zeke's money at once with knockout drops.

Zeke had felt young and free then. He hadn't killed a man. He was just a good-looking, go-to-hell puncher with a summer's wages to spend, a crooked grin on his face and his blond hair standing straight up with devilment. He hadn't meant anybody any harm.

The bartender had put too many in the slug and Zeke had tasted it. That had begun the long trail. It stood like yesterday between Zeke and the street, a painful haze of circumstance out of which a few details moved clear.

Mesa was a crooked town. It had sprung up with a railroad and it fought its fights from ambush. It was a cloud of wickedness on the clean range. That was what the preacher had said and he had been right. Gamblers, women, toughs had settled at this final end-of-line which stopped two spans of railroad tracks head-on to span a continent. Few punchers had been there. Zeke had been drifting south from Wyoming. He had not intended to stay beyond the night. But he had tasted the Mickey Finn and he had thrown the glass straight into the bartender's face.

The fight had been brief. Zeke had gone half over the bar to punish his man, when a loafing tough, anxious for a drink, took sides and a chair from behind. Zeke Tomlin was stretched out in the sawdust.

Les Harmon had come in and his star looked big. He had taken Zeke's gun and with some help had dragged him to the nearby *calabozo* where the cell door had clanged.

Zeke lay for some time in the dark. He had had a little to drink and he had swallowed some of the Mickey. He did not immediately become aware of the voices in the sheriff's office. Then: "All right," he heard one say. "They're too sore about their payroll for us to take chances. But it sounds kind of crazy just the same."

"Take him and do like I said!" said Harmon with a strange eagerness.

A blustering big man, black-booted and frock-coated with a yard of string tie, opened the door. "Hey, sonny," the big man had said. "If you want to get out of here, you can give us a hand."

"I'm stayin'," said Zeke.

One of the hard cases with the big man said, "Shall we persuade him, Big George?"

Big George nodded and they stood Zeke up, three of them, and shoved him out to his horse. Zeke saw Les Harmon's hard, cold face under the kerosene lamp in the office. Les Harmon was faintly amused.

They put Zeke on a horse and tied his legs to the cinch and led him out of town through the shadows. The yellow squares of light lay behind them in the desert when they halted at last.

"Gag him," said Big George.

Zeke glared but they gagged him, tight so that it was hard to breathe. Then they passed the bridle off his horse and let Zeke have his hands.

"It's about ten," said Big George, looking at the stars. "She won't be along for another half-hour."

Zeke saw then they were beside a faint road. The group was looking back at the town, sitting tensely, fussing with their reins.

"Hope nobody starts in from the mine," said somebody.

"They won't," said Big George. "The boss won't let them off until they get their full week's work out. They don't think they'll get their pay and nobody is liable to quit without it."

One of the owl-hoots snickered nervously. "They'll have to wait longer than that."

"Shut up," said Big George.

It was cold and the desert wind was sharp through Zeke's shirt. The stars snapped brilliantly in their countless millions. The horses moved restively back and forth around the boulder which Big George had taken for his station.

"All right," said Big George, looking for his clock amongst the stars. "You and Eddy climb down and take them from the right side of the trail. Bill, you and Oofty take cover behind this rock. Mike, take the horses and get back out of range."

They had snapped a lead rope on Zeke's mount. Big George led it off the trail and stood there, waiting. The desert wind was blowing colder through Zeke's shirt. He heard the man called Mike taking the horses well off the trail and then hoofclicks over dry, hard stone. There was a riverbed near at hand.

It was terribly dark. The stars in their brilliance made the earth seem blacker. The smell of sage was keen in the cold air.

Something was coming from town now. The far-off rumble grew louder and the ground began to tremble under the pound of hoofs and coach wheels. It was traveling dark and traveling fast.

It came nearer. Suddenly from both sides of the trail flame spat. The two lead horses, shot squarely, were two wrenching screams in the night. A shouting confusion swelled up with the unseen dust. More guns blasted, orange and blinding.

Men swore. One last shot sounded and a groan died out. The man called Bill rode up.

"They won't tell nobody nothin' now," said Bill.

"You sure?" said Big George.

"Sure I'm sure," said Bill.

"Take this rope," said Big George and rode toward the wrecked stage. Presently one final shot sounded and Big George came back. "You'd bungle everything if I didn't wipe your noses for you. You got the pouch, Mike?"

"I got it," said Oofty.

"Let's ride," said Bill nervously.

"Not so fast," said Big George. "All right, you."

He took hold of Zeke's gag and ripped it loose. He hung the bridle on Zeke's pommel.

Zeke said nothing. He knew it wouldn't do any good.

"Give me that pouch," said Big George. He took a sheaf of bills from it, and stuffed several by the edge under the cinch of Zeke's saddle. Big George tested the lashings which secured Zeke's legs and then put on two new ones, lower down.

Zeke's horse began to tremble. Big George was shoving something under the saddle blanket.

"You take my advice," said Big George, "and ride! The sheriff will be here in about twenty minutes. He'll have a few friends and they'll be plenty mad when they see them horses. The sheriff will shoot you on sight. My advice is ride."

He slashed the mount's rump with his knife and the horse leaped forward. A quirt popped and the horse began to run, blindly, crazily, splitting the cold desert wind.

Crazy with the cut and whatever was under the blanket—driven down by each leap—the horse reached across the range, slashing through sage, stumbling and springing up again.

Zeke knew why he was there now. To make a trail while the others took a streambed. He knew why Les Harmon had given up a prisoner. Sometime since, the sheriff would have been "surprised" by the far-off gunfire and would have ridden forth with the mine company's friends in town. It was coldblooded, it would work. They must have done it before.

The maddened horse raced on. They would count on Zeke's attempts to free himself. He determined he would not. Let the mine company find him as he was.

And then the horse nearly plunged off a cliff and went careening over a slide. Zeke began to contort himself to get at the lashings on his legs and feet.

He slashed the mount's rump with his knife and the horse leaped forward. A quirt popped and the horse began to run, blindly, crazily, splitting the cold desert wind.

The horse had obviously not come from town. He had no destination. He was running with pain and whatever was under the saddle blanket. Zeke got the lashings off one leg. And then fate at once hurt and helped him.

The horse went into a hole and the snap of its breaking leg was loud. It fell on its neck and toward the side Zeke had freed. Stunned, Zeke rose in a little while from the dead mount and unwound the lashings from his other leg.

He was unsteady and sick, badly shaken and scared. He thought he could hear hoofbeats off somewhere. He would have no defense. Les Harmon was riding up to kill him and solve a robbery.

Zeke felt under the cinch. The implanted bills were gone, strewn back to make a trail. How far he had come and just where the holdup lay, Zeke did not know. He knew he had to have a gun. There were guns back there with the dead men.

He skirted his dead horse and climbed over hard rock to a ridge. He stood and looked and found the lights of Mesa. He was not sure of his landmarks but he had some vague recollection of where north had been at the holdup and where the town had lain.

He wondered if he dared approach the town. He could try to tell them about Harmon and Big George. But it came to him suddenly that he was a stranger in town. Who would know him or believe him? He was just a puncher on the loose with his summer's pay. A stranger in town.

Zeke walked the ridge, listening over his heartbeats to the sigh of the desert wind. Pursuit would come to him sooner or later.

Then he recalled that there might be a horse at the holdup and he walked faster.

About an hour later he crossed the trail. He looked intently at the lights of the town and tried to judge whether they were further or nearer than the holdup. They seemed smaller but distance was deceptive in this clear air and he had gone almost a mile before he knew that he had guessed wrong. He was well off the trail, staying on rocks where he could. He went back. He was getting nervous. By this time several people would be around the wreck. He was certain of this. If they'd left a gun—

He had guessed right about the people. There were lanterns bobbing and even at a distance one could see the bodies under the blankets, beside the broken wheels of the coach. There were lots of legs around the lanterns, throwing long, thick shadows outward from the scene.

Zeke kept to the sage and watched. Once he heard somebody shout to an approaching rider, "You get him, Harmon?"

"This ain't Harmon. I come back with my horse lame. They got his trail."

"Funny, just one man."

"There mighta been more. Harmon says it was probably just one. They'll have him before mornin'! Harmon says it mighta been that waddy that tried to bust up Sloppy Joe. He heered about the coach load and got hisself out of jail. Sawed the bars."

"Young, tow-headed kid in a red shirt?"

"That's him. Harmon says to kill him on sight. He's wanted in ten states and five territories."

"Seems funny, just one man. Ground looks like it's been dragged around here."

"You ain't got no Apache in you, Blucher. Shut up."

"Still, seems funny."

"Harmon says to shoot him on sight."

"I think he had friends."

"He ain't got no friends. He's just some owl-hoot stranger."

"Let's get back to town. I'm dry. Harmon's got five men with him."

"I'm sticking around to see what happens."

They continued to remain around the coach. Somebody built a fire. The night wind stiffened.

Zeke gave it up. He was shivering with nervousness and cold, and he knew it would be daylight before long. Suddenly he felt himself getting mad.

Zeke got up and walked to the dry riverbed. He cast up and down it for some time, feeling rocks, not daring to strike a light. Suddenly he became interested. His questing fingers had found a rough place on a stone where the riverbed narrowed, upstream from the holdup. He walked rapidly then, sure of the distance of Big George from the scene of the murders. He got madder as he walked. He had no slightest notion of what he would do. He kept on walking.

Somewhere ahead would be Big George.

It was dawn and Zeke was still walking. It was easier now to catch these occasional chips from the stone and the very rare prints in the sand patches, but it was terribly dangerous now that Big George might look back.

Zeke kept on walking. At noon he found a muddied pool

and drank heavily from it, sure now that Big George could not be far ahead of him. He was getting even madder.

In midafternoon he walked with less spring. It was getting heavier, this stone going, and the riverbed was rising sharply into the hills. If it had been alive, he would have died where he was from a bullet.

A shirt was barely showing in a crevice. They had stoned a man out of sight. Zeke pulled away the gray boulders and found the body of a hard-faced young man. The wound was old and it had bled a lot. Then Big George's people had not entirely escaped in the holdup. He didn't know if this was Mike or Oofty or who. He could not recall their names. But they had buried him where he had died. Ten minutes' more work and Zeke sat down in disappointment. They had buried this man but they had taken his guns.

Zeke put the stones in place and went on up the riverbed. Here, in the wet season, cascades had fallen. The going got harder and the climb more steep and it was nightfall before the stream began to branch and dwindle.

Hungry and thirsty to the point of torment, Zeke threw himself down on the bank of the dry stream and rested. He did not know this country. His horse and his gear were gone. He had no weapons and he was hunted.

He walked now by the faint light of the quarter moon which would soon be gone and his way was slow because he had to locate tracks each time the dry bed forked.

It was midnight when he found water and he drank it in great gulps, trying to stop himself but unable to repress the tremendous greed of his thirst. He was sick for a short time and then began to feel better. Some courage came back into him.

Suddenly he sat up and asked himself what he was doing here. It was a queer sensation. Like a man waking from a nightmare and finding it was real. What was he doing here?

He tried to piece back over his logic without effect. So shocked had he been after the fall that he could not even remember what had happened when he left the holdup. Vaguely he remembered feeling angry and smart. The last place Harmon would permit anybody to look was on the track of Big George. That thought must have been with him. It was all animal cunning, hardly rational at all, the cleverness of the hunted, the fox doubling his tracks to elude the pack. But he had no gun to front Big George and Big George had guns and men.

Even if he went back and tried to tell them that Big George had done the robbery, they would shoot him down. Those men had been furious with the killing of the coach horses and the men they knew. And Zeke was just a stranger in town.

But he had no other way to go and he could not retrace what he had so arduously won in distance. The moon was gone sometime since but he had stopped looking for Big George's tracks. All he wanted to do was get out of the country.

After some interminable time—an hour—he heard the running of water and came at length to the edge of a stream which was encased by cliffs. He had passed the divide of the hills. The old streamed he had traveled had once carried some of the burden of this present river. He sensed himself in a tumbled, dangerous country and the roar of the water in the deep gorge was frightening, deep and savage.

For an hour or more he felt his way along the canyon rim, trying to find a way down. It was dangerous work in the darkness. He finally stopped and rested. It was then he saw the pinpoint of light through trees.

Hope came up to him. He had money. He could perhaps buy a horse and a gun and a canteen and food. Perhaps he had a chance now. He went eagerly toward the light.

It was a hut, closed about by rocks and pines, situated on a tiny creek. Zeke moved more rapidly toward it. He came to the door and raised his fist to knock.

An instant before his knuckles struck he heard, "To hell with Harmon, I say. It's an easy ride to New Mexico!" It was the voice of Big George and Big George was drunk.

"I don't like to chance it," said Oofty. "He's half bloodhound. You see him the night he killed Sammy Walker? By God, his eyes! He's death-hungry, I tell you. He'd rather hunt down a man for the kill than eat. I swear he would. I ain't runnin' out without makin' sure he gets at least some of his share."

"You're a fool!" roared Big George.

"Hell, that ain't no secret," said Mike. "I ain't afraid of Harmon. Pass me the bottle. He's a hog, wantin' half. Who's afraid of Harmon?"

"I am," said Bill. "He's kill-crazy. You think it's just the good idea of it that made him figure out a man to hunt. He loves it. The idea is loony. I said many a time if the hoss stumbled, there'd be a man tied up and pinned down. Harmon likes to hunt. I'm fer splittin' like he wants and gettin' more."

"No more in this country," said Big George. "I'm through with it. Too condemned dangerous. We don't need Harmon. We got thirty thousand dollars last night. Fifteen won't split far. I ain't afraid of Harmon. Drink up."

"I'm scared," said Eddy. "It's like Oofty says. We got Pete's share now. Let's be square with Harmon. Harmon's squirrely in the skull about huntin' men. That ain't no lie about why he thunk up this false trail. He told me once, 'Eddy, you ever git hungry?' And I said, 'Hell, yes.' 'You know how it kind of gnaws you?' he says. 'Sure,' I says, with no idea what he was talkin' about. 'That's the way it is with me sometimes,' he says. 'Eat,' I says, bein' practical. 'I ain't talkin' about food, Eddy,' he says. Harmon made us turn that young puncher loose just so he could have the fun of killin' him. Wasn't no *other* sense to it."

"Well, let him have that for his pay," said Big George.

"That's all right for you that can throw lead like you—You hear something?" Oofty got up.

Zeke had made no sound. But one of the staked horses had overturned a wash pan some gold miner had left in the creek.

Big George came outside with his gun cocked, swiftly sidestepped from the light of the door and stood still, listening. The horse overturned the pan again and Big George uncocked his gun and went in.

"Give me a drink," he said, kicking the door shut.

81

Stepping out from the shadow of the wall, Zeke began to breathe again. He moved to get around back of the building and stumbled on some riding equipment. The noise passed without notice from within and Zeke was about to move on when his shin struck the stock of a rifle still in its boot. It was a Winchester.

Some of Zeke's strength came back. He drew the rifle forth and fingered it for its load. The magazine was full and ten extra cartridges were in loops on the side of the boot.

He did not know immediately what he would do with it. Coldblooded murder was not in his line. And yet . . .

They continued their drinking in the hut and began to wrangle once more about the split. Big George was so heated that he offered to pay Oofty and Eddy their shares but they would not be a party to defection. It would cause disaster to fall on them too certainly. Big George then offered them the larger part of the cut and they, drunker, became abusive.

Zeke did not know who struck the first blow. There was a crash and the light went out and then a man came stumbling outside swearing while furniture broke within. A moment later Zeke had made up his mind. He stepped to the door and fired blindly into the tumult. There was a scream. Zeke threw himself along the base of the house.

Three more shots sounded and Big George, raving and cursing, came outside, shooting at anything which moved.

Two shots came from the door and Big George dropped to one knee and shot at the flame. Oofty folded up and began to cough, dry and hard. Somebody was running away in the darkness and Big George lurched after him.

"Come back with that pouch!" shouted Big George.

A shot came back at him and Big George returned it and kept on going. The sound of a scuffle came from the direction of the river and grew distant. And then there was a scream, a long, dwindling yell which was to haunt Zeke through his days.

Somebody came back from the direction of the river. It was not Big George.

"Oofty!" he called. It was Eddy. Oofty was coughing, dry and hard.

"He went over the edge with it!" said Eddy in a scared voice. "I was goin' to take it back to Harmon and he went over the edge with it. It's gone in the canyon. We got to ride and fast. Harmon won't never believe us!"

Oofty kept coughing, growing weaker.

A footstep sounded inside the door. "You condemned dog," said Bill in a cold, emotionless voice. "You've done for us all!" And he fired straight into Eddy's chest.

Bill walked out to the horses and began to saddle one. He came back and got a pair of canteens, the gunnysack which contained their food and an extra rifle. He mounted up and quirted away from there.

Oofty was not coughing.

Zeke lay there for a long time, listening for Eddy or Mike to move. The half-light before dawn came and fell on the dew-wet face of Eddy, staring sightlessly upwards.

Zeke found Mike inside, not very pretty. Zeke took the remaining supplies outside and put them in a saddlebag. He filled up the canteens at a spring.

After he had saddled, despite his haste to get away, he went to the edge of the canyon rim and looked down at the water. It was a straight drop but it ended in a beach. The body of Big George was lying there small and crumpled two hundred feet down.

Zeke found toeholds the cabin's builder had cut in the cliff and went down along the side of the silvery rivulet which dropped in small falls from the spring above. He looked up and down the beach and behind rocks. If the pouch had been there he would have seen it. It was not.

He stood for a little while looking at the river. It was deep and angry and red and went into a gorge just below which made it steeply waved and boiling. The pouch, he knew, would never be found.

He did not know how tired he was until he tried to climb the cliff once more. It took him a long time to reach the top and when he got there he lay face downward in the wet grass. How many hours had it been since he slept?

He was to know many more.

He was in the act of mounting when the bullet took him in the leg. He whirled to see Les Harmon, a hundred yards down the rim, coming fast, hungry eyes above a lathered horse.

Zeke made it up. He jabbed spur and his horse leaped eastward and away from Harmon. Zeke plied quirt and rode low. Bullets smacked into trees and showered him with needles as he raced.

His horse was fresh. He had water. Harmon would have to stop and change mounts. Zeke rode.

That had been nine months ago, nine months of jumping at sharp sounds in the night, of waking up to hear Oofty coughing dry and hard again, seeing Harmon's eyes.

And there was Harmon's horse before the Golden Horn while Harmon was inside. And between the sight and Zeke drifted the haze of remembrance. Zeke put down the gun rag. He was beginning to shake. He knew what the kill-hungry eyes looked like.

Les Harmon stood for a moment at the Golden Horn's swinging doors and a sleepy Mexican pointed out the hardware store. Les Harmon nodded briefly and came down the steps to walk through the white, dry dust. He was slow, casual, certain, tasting the flavor of it.

Zeke opened the breech of the buffalo gun and started to put in a shell. It was the wrong caliber. He fumbled for the box and tore it getting a .50 cartridge out. He thrust it into the foul breech of the weapon and had just closed it when Harmon was standing in the door, gun in his hand, star on his chest.

"Hello, Tomlin!"

The hot afternoon was cold. The buffalo gun lay unraised on the counter. Zeke tried to speak, cleared his throat and tried again.

"What do you want?"

Harmon juggled the gun in his hand and spun it, bringing it up center on Zeke's chest. His eyes were cold, cold and gray white. They looked hungry.

"I think you got some information for me, Tomlin."

"I . . . I haven't got anything from you. For you."

"Now, it's funny, but I think you have. Tomlin, there's thirty thousand dollars that you know about."

"It went over the rim with Big George."

Harmon looked his contempt. He gazed around the shop. "Nobody here, that's convenient."

Zeke tried to think.

"Now I wouldn't try anything foolish," said Harmon. "I can shoot before you can begin to move that gun. What did you do with the thirty thousand, Tomlin?"

Zeke licked dry lips. Harmon's eyes were like a snake's, hypnotic. They were hungry. "You ever find the last man of that gang?"

"Never looked," said Harmon.

"How . . . how'd you find me?"

"Drummer. Said somebody way down here was askin' for me. Described you. That simple. But it took a long time, Tomlin. A long time. I got tired waitin'. Awful tired, Tomlin. Where's the money?"

"It went over the rim with Big George!"

"Now Tomlin, you're bein' foolish, boy. You're a stranger in this town. Mex said so. You don't mix much—a little poker. You're a stranger. They don't know nothin' about you. Me, I'm sheriff. You resisted arrest, that's all. Formalities ain't too strict. It's been a long hunt, Tomlin. An awful long hunt."

Zeke knew he was right. But he stopped shaking. This was it. If he shot it out here, even then they'd kill him for murdering a lawman. They'd call it that. But this was it. The whole haze of memory and the throbbing of his leg took him and passed over him and he was cold but calm.

"Big George went into the river with it, Harmon. You ride out of here."

Harmon's expression didn't change. He took a step nearer.

Suddenly Zeke ducked and swung the gun. A lamp to the right of his head spattered in silver fragments. The store was full of sound. The unshouldered buffalo gun sprang out of Zeke's grasp and split its butt on the wall.

There was silence in the room. One of Zeke's fingers was bleeding where the recoil of the .50 caliber had torn it. He fumbled for a second cartridge in the box and through the glass of the case saw Harmon's boot.

There was not much left of the lawman's chest. His left breast was a hole where a mushroom slug as big as a thumb had gone.

Les Harmon was dead.

Zeke stood up. They would hang him now. Hang him sure. Hang him because he was a stranger to them.

The proprietor came dazedly in from the rooms in the rear where he had been taking his siesta. The front doors burst inwards and Tom Brennerman was there, star big and bright.

They would take him away now, thought Zeke.

Tom Brennerman looked at Harmon and rolled the face over with the toe of his boot. He looked for a little while and then turned to thrust back interested citizenry.

"You all right, Zeke?" said Tom Brennerman.

Zeke looked amazedly at the marshal.

"You sure drilled him clean, Zeke," said McTavish who owned the store. "And you give him the first shot!"

"You all right, Zeke?" demanded the marshal again.

"Yeah. Yeah, I'm all right," said Zeke.

"You better go lie down, you're that white," said Brennerman. "Make him lie down and give him a drink, McTavish. Them buffaler guns kick a man somethin' fierce."

"You come on and lie down and have a drink," said McTavish.

Somebody in the street said, "Zeke all right?"

A curious voice piped up from the door, "Who was it shot at Zeke?"

Brennerman glanced at the body which two men were gathering up. He shrugged. Bending over, he looked through the dead man's pockets. There was nothing to identify him.

"Dunno," said Brennerman. "Anybody can wear a star. That don't necessarily make him a sheriff. Nothin' here to say who he is. Looks like we'll never know. Just some stranger in town, lookin' for trouble."

Zeke permitted himself to be led into the back room. McTavish made him comfortable on a bed and beamed at him.

"That . . . that dead man," began Zeke, "is a lawman . . ."

"Och! Zeke boy, we have had others try to pull that trick on us before. They come in here with a badge and try to settle old feuds in the name of the law of some faraway town. We're not so innocent. You heard what Brennerman said, didn't you? 'Just a stranger in town.' We know you; we don't know him."

Zeke smiled and a deep, beautiful peace began to settle down over him. McTavish patted his shoulder and went to find a refill from his private stock.

Zeke knew the term "stranger" no longer applied to him.

STORY PREVIEW

NOW that you've just ventured through some of the captivating tales in the Stories from the Golden Age collection by L. Ron Hubbard, turn the page and enjoy a preview of *Shadows from Boot Hill*. Join outlaw Brazos as he races to take a "hit job" from Whisper Monahan. But things soon take a supernatural spin when Brazos acquires another shadow after killing a witch doctor, who, with his last breath, swears a deadly curse upon his soul.

SHADOWS FROM BOOT HILL

ON a hot afternoon in August, Brazos chased his shadow toward Los Hornos at a speed which indicated that all the devils from hell and maybe even some angels were hot upon him. He fled with more fury than fright, for it seemed to him that the murder of a banker ought to be considered in the light of public good. Too, he nursed a feeling of grievance, for the law had been so swift and determined that he had not even had time to collect the five hundred dollars in double eagles which was to have been his pay for the job. The buckskin money belt was damp and light beneath his buckskin shirt, just as both Peacemaker and Martini-Henry were empty at belt and saddle side.

And this was a hell of a country to try to get lost in.

And Los Hornos, ahead, was about as safe a sanctuary as a barrel of sidewinders.

Brazos swore at his luck, swore at his horse and swore at his shadow. He cursed the sage, he cursed the dust and he spat into the unoffending eye of a horned toad by the way. If he had good sense he'd larrup south to the border, but if he had better sense he'd crack a Wells Fargo safe before he went—for visitors in the land of the *dons* were welcome in proportion to their purses. It was like Brazos to barely keep a posse's dust under the rim of the world behind and consider ways of replenishing his exchequer.

Los Hornos came writhing into sight amid its heat waves, moving slowly up in mirage as though somebody had a jack under the town and then dropping suddenly, as though the jack had slipped. Behind it, red sandstone buttes appeared ready for the frying pan; all around it, dusty sage drooped in drab boredom; in it, the inhabitants were following a theory that a fiery sun without was best combated by firewater within.

Brazos looked over his shoulder in anxiety. The posse thought he would have to head for Los Hornos, and the posse had a couple of Apache trackers along to confirm its guess. And this horse, which he had stolen from a sheepherder (which didn't make it theft) wouldn't last another league. He had to stop in Los Hornos or be stopped. His quirt fell and the weary mustang sped along.

Who did he know in Los Hornos? Only one man. Whisper Monahan. A slight shudder of premonition went over Brazos and, because he believed in premonition, he did not take the symptom in a good light. The last time he'd worked for Whisper Monahan they had not parted the best of friends. But a posse is a posse, and a half friend is better than an enemy with gun smoke in his fist, and so Brazos went streaming into the main street of Los Hornos.

A couple of Indian dogs leaped out of slumber and from under his hoofs with dismal yelps. A loafer in the shade of the store porch went right on sleeping. There was a sign, "Star Livery Stable, Whisper Monahan, Prop." Brazos swung the horse, and the moist warmth and dimness of the stable swallowed him.

In the office, Whisper Monahan and a hostler named Henry looked languidly at the opening door and then came fully awake. For a few seconds the silence was very deep. Whisper Monahan was built close to the ground, and not all the sun in the Southwest could have turned his pasty pallor into anything but a pasty pallor. But, awkward and scared as he seemed, he always got what he wanted, no matter the methods he had to use.

Brazos was inclined to be truculent. He wasn't very tall, but he wasn't very thick, either, and when men first looked at him they thought him a forceful and powerful individual. His mouth was almost at forty-five degrees with his face, and his eyes proclaimed a dislike for the world. And now, with his buckskin stained and his flat Texas hat gray with dust and his much-used—if at present empty—gun at his side, he looked ready to take on a regiment, having just finished off a brigade.

"Hello, Brazos."

"Hello, Whisper."

"You come far and fast, Brazos."

"I come with half the citizens of Tulos on my heels."

"Well, now, Brazos, that's too bad. What happened?"

"I killed a gent that needed killing, and I didn't even collect the double eagles. This country is goin' to hell for keeps."

"Yeah. The law is gettin' the upper hand, worse luck."

"You gotta cover me, Whisper."

"Why?"

"Because I said you gotta."

Whisper grinned suddenly inside himself. "That's too bad, Brazos. But I reckon you just better keep riding."

"My hoss is half dead and I ain't goin' to keep riding."

"Then you better start walking, Brazos."

"You can't do this to me!"

"You ain't got a cartridge left in your belt and most likely none in your gun. You better be goin', Brazos, afore them fellers come streaking in here and string you up."

"You can't do this to me!"

"I'm doin' it, Brazos."

"But they'll kill me!"

Whisper was laughing inside himself now, though he looked very contrite and sorrowful. Brazos wore a silver cross on a silver chain around his neck, and when Brazos got pushed to it he generally fingered the cross in hopes it would bring him luck. Whisper saw him doing it, and knew that he had his man.

"Too bad," said Whisper. "You better be goin' afore they get here."

"Now look, Whisper! Ain't you always been my friend?"

"I've hired you once in a while," said Whisper.

"Well, hire me again! I need help, and I need it bad!"

"Hire you? Shucks, I haven't got anything for you to do."

"Sure you have, Whisper!"

Whisper was hard put to keep looking thoughtful. Finally he scrubbed at his bald head and spoke doubtfully. "Well—I could get you to kill Scotty Brant for me, but you wouldn't do that."

"Sure I would, Whisper! You gotta help me."

"Well—just as a favor to you, I'll let you do it. I'll even pay you a couple hundred for the job."

"That's white!" cried Brazos in relief. "I knew you'd help me."

Whisper had won and he threw off his lethargy. "Henry, you saddle up Beans and ride hell for leather for the buttes. About dark you cut back, take to the bed of Dead River to cover your trail and come home."

About an hour later Brazos was lying in the mow, not daring to breathe while Whisper "discovered" with shocked alarm that he had aided the escape of a criminal. But shortly Brazos breathed again, for the posse, hot for blood, went thundering out of town on the trail of Beans and Henry, flailing their jaded mounts and licking their chops as they envisioned the riddled corpse of one Brazos.

Whisper stood in the door watching them become a cloud of dust. Whisper, down inside, was laughing, but not at the joke he had played on the posse.

To find out more about *Shadows from Boot Hill* and how you can obtain your copy, go to www.goldenagestories.com.

GLOSSARY

GLOSSARY

STORIES FROM THE GOLDEN AGE *reflect the words and expressions used in the 1930s and 1940s, adding unique flavor and authenticity to the tales. While a character's speech may often reflect regional origins, it also can convey attitudes common in the day. So that readers can better grasp such cultural and historical terms, uncommon words or expressions of the era, the following glossary has been provided.*

---

alkali: a powdery white mineral that salts the ground in many low places in the West. It whitens the ground where water has risen to the surface and gone back down.

bead on, take a: to take careful aim at. This term alludes to the *bead*, a small metal knob on a firearm used as a front sight.

blamed: confounded.

blue chip: a poker chip having a high value.

boot: saddle boot; a close-fitting covering or case for a gun or other weapon that straps to a saddle.

buffalo gun: .50-caliber Sharps rifle, also called the "Big Fifty," which weighed twelve pounds. Noted for its power and range, it was the almost unanimous choice among buffalo hunters. The drawbacks were the cost of ammunition and the fact that the rifle's accuracy was seriously affected by rapid fire (it had to be watered down constantly to keep from overheating).

calabozo: (Spanish) jail.

Colt: a single-action, six-shot cylinder revolver, most commonly available in .45- or .44-caliber versions. It was first manufactured in 1873 for the Army by the Colt Firearms Company, the armory founded by American inventor Samuel Colt (1814–1862) who revolutionized the firearms industry with the invention of the revolver. The Colt, also known as the Peacemaker, was also made available to civilians. As a reliable, inexpensive and popular handgun among cowboys, it became known as the "cowboy's gun" and a symbol of the Old West.

cowpuncher: a hired hand who tends cattle and performs other duties on horseback.

Derringer: a pocket-sized, short-barreled, large-caliber pistol. Named for the US gunsmith Henry Deringer (1786–1868), who designed it.

drag: the rear of a column of cattle on the trail. It includes the footsore, the weak, the young calves, the weary and the lazy. The drag position is no fun for the hands assigned to ride it—they have to make the sick and the stragglers keep up, chase the breakaways and suffer the dust. Since it is unpleasant, green hands usually get assigned to ride drag.

fan: to fire a series of shots (from a single-action revolver) by holding the trigger back and successively striking the hammer to the rear with the free hand.

Giant: Giant powder; dynamite manufactured by the Giant Powder Co, the first US dynamite manufacturing plant, in 1870 in San Francisco, California. "Giant powder" was a long time synonym for dynamite in the US.

gig: a light carriage, with one pair of wheels, drawn by one horse.

G-men: government men; agents of the Federal Bureau of Investigation.

gumbo: soil that turns very sticky and muddy when it becomes wet; found throughout the central US.

half-breed: a person with parents of different races, usually a white father and Native American mother. The term originated in the East, not the Western frontier.

hoss: horse.

hostler: a person who takes care of horses, especially at an inn.

jenny: a female donkey.

jimminies, by: a mild exclamation of surprise, emotion or awe.

larrup: to beat, flog or thrash, said of a horse to make it go faster.

livery stable: a stable that accommodates and looks after horses for their owners.

Martini-Henry: a breech-loaded .45-caliber rifle adopted in 1871 as the standard British service weapon, named after its inventors.

Mickey Finn: a drug-laced drink given to someone without their knowledge in order to incapacitate them. Named after a bartender who, before his days as a saloon proprietor, was known as a pickpocket and thief who often preyed on drunken bar patrons.

mow: haymow; the upper floor of a barn or stable used for storing hay.

owl-hoot: outlaw.

parley: to talk or negotiate, especially with an enemy.

Peacemaker: nickname for the single-action (that is, cocked by hand for each shot), six-shot Army model revolver first produced in 1873 by the Colt Firearms Company, the armory founded by Samuel Colt (1814–1862). The handgun of the Old West, it became the instrument of both lawmaker and lawbreaker during the last twenty-five years of the nineteenth century. It soon earned various names, such as "hog leg," "Equalizer," and "Judge Colt and his jury of six."

placer: a waterborne deposit of gravel or sand containing heavy ore minerals, as gold, which have been eroded from their original bedrock and concentrated as small particles that can be washed out.

poke: a small sack or bag, usually a crude leather pouch, in which a miner carried his gold dust and nuggets.

Prop.: Proprietor.

puncher: a hired hand who tends cattle and performs other duties on horseback.

quirt: a riding whip with a short handle and a braided leather lash.

rannies: ranahans; cowboys or top ranch hands.

riffles: in mining, the strips of metal or wooden slats fixed to the bottom of a rocker box or sluice (a long sloping trough into which water is directed), that run perpendicular to the flow of water. The weight of the gold causes it to sink, where it is captured by these riffles.

Scheherazade: the female narrator of *The Arabian Nights,* who during one thousand and one adventurous nights saved her life by entertaining her husband, the king, with stories.

sidewinder: rattlesnake.

sinks: depressions in the land surface where water has no outlet and simply stands. The word is usually applied to dry lake beds, where the evaporating water has left alkali and other mineral salts.

slug: a bullet.

sluice: sluice box; a long, narrow wood or metal artificial channel that water passes through when put in a creek or stream to separate the dirt and junk material away from the gold. Gold, a very dense metal, stays in the sluice box because of its heavy weight.

"Streets of Laredo": a song, also known as the "Cowboy's Lament." It is a famous cowboy ballad in which a dying cowboy dispenses his advice to another.

trail herd: a herd of cattle driven along a trail, especially from their home range to market.

waddy: a cowboy, especially one who drifts from ranch to ranch and helps out in busy times. In the spring and fall when some ranches were short-handed, they took on anyone who was able to ride a horse and used him for a week or so; hence the word *waddy,* derived from *wadding*—anything to fill in. Some cowmen used the word to mean a cattle rustler; later it was applied to any cowboy.

war sack: a cowboy's bag for his personal possessions, plunder, cartridges, etc. Often made of canvas but sometimes just a flour or grain sack, it is usually tied behind the saddle.

Winchester: an early family of repeating rifles; a single-barreled rifle containing multiple rounds of ammunition. Manufactured by the Winchester Repeating Arms Company, it was widely used in the US during the latter half of the nineteenth century. The 1873 model is often called "the gun that won the West" for its immense popularity at that time, as well as its use in fictional Westerns.

wind devils: spinning columns of air that move across the landscape and pick up loose dust. They look like miniature tornados, but are not as powerful.

Yucatán: a peninsula mostly in southeastern Mexico between the Caribbean Sea and the Gulf of Mexico.

L. Ron Hubbard
in the Golden Age
of Pulp Fiction

*In writing an adventure story
a writer has to know that he is adventuring
for a lot of people who cannot.
The writer has to take them here and there
about the globe and show them
excitement and love and realism.
As long as that writer is living the part of an
adventurer when he is hammering
the keys, he is succeeding with his story.*

*Adventuring is a state of mind.
If you adventure through life, you have a
good chance to be a success on paper.*

*Adventure doesn't mean globe-trotting,
exactly, and it doesn't mean great deeds.
Adventuring is like art.
You have to live it to make it real.*

—L. RON HUBBARD

L. Ron Hubbard
and American
Pulp Fiction

B ORN March 13, 1911, L. Ron Hubbard lived a life at least as expansive as the stories with which he enthralled a hundred million readers through a fifty-year career.

Originally hailing from Tilden, Nebraska, he spent his formative years in a classically rugged Montana, replete with the cowpunchers, lawmen and desperadoes who would later people his Wild West adventures. And lest anyone imagine those adventures were drawn from vicarious experience, he was not only breaking broncs at a tender age, he was also among the few whites ever admitted into Blackfoot society as a bona fide blood brother. While if only to round out an otherwise rough and tumble youth, his mother was that rarity of her time—a thoroughly educated woman—who introduced her son to the classics of Occidental literature even before his seventh birthday.

But as any dedicated L. Ron Hubbard reader will attest, his world extended far beyond Montana. In point of fact, and as the son of a United States naval officer, by the age of eighteen he had traveled over a quarter of a million miles. Included therein were three Pacific crossings to a then still mysterious Asia, where he ran with the likes of Her British Majesty's agent-in-place

for North China, and the last in the line of Royal Magicians from the court of Kublai Khan. For the record, L. Ron Hubbard was also among the first Westerners to gain admittance to forbidden Tibetan monasteries below Manchuria, and his photographs of China's Great Wall long graced American geography texts.

L. Ron Hubbard, left, at Congressional Airport, Washington, DC, 1931, with members of George Washington University flying club.

Upon his return to the United States and a hasty completion of his interrupted high school education, the young Ron Hubbard entered George Washington University. There, as fans of his aerial adventures may have heard, he earned his wings as a pioneering barnstormer at the dawn of American aviation. He also earned a place in free-flight record books for the longest sustained flight above Chicago. Moreover, as a roving reporter for *Sportsman Pilot* (featuring his first professionally penned articles), he further helped inspire a generation of pilots who would take America to world airpower.

Immediately beyond his sophomore year, Ron embarked on the first of his famed ethnological expeditions, initially to then untrammeled Caribbean shores (descriptions of which would later fill a whole series of West Indies mystery-thrillers). That the Puerto Rican interior would also figure into the future of Ron Hubbard stories was likewise no accident. For in addition to cultural studies of the island, a 1932–33

LRH expedition is rightly remembered as conducting the first complete mineralogical survey of a Puerto Rico under United States jurisdiction.

There was many another adventure along this vein: As a lifetime member of the famed Explorers Club, L. Ron Hubbard charted North Pacific waters with the first shipboard radio direction finder, and so pioneered a long-range navigation system universally employed until the late twentieth century. While not to put too fine an edge on it, he also held a rare Master Mariner's license to pilot any vessel, of any tonnage in any ocean.

Yet lest we stray too far afield, there is an LRH note at this juncture in his saga, and it reads in part:

"I started out writing for the pulps, writing the best I knew, writing for every mag on the stands, slanting as well as I could."

To which one might add: His earliest submissions date from the summer of 1934, and included tales drawn from true-to-life Asian adventures, with characters roughly modeled on British/American intelligence operatives he had known in Shanghai. His early Westerns were similarly peppered with details drawn from personal experience. Although therein lay a first hard lesson from the often cruel world of the pulps. His first Westerns were soundly rejected as lacking the authenticity of a Max Brand yarn

Capt. L. Ron Hubbard in Ketchikan, Alaska, 1940, on his Alaskan Radio Experimental Expedition, the first of three voyages conducted under the Explorers Club flag.

(a particularly frustrating comment given L. Ron Hubbard's Westerns came straight from his Montana homeland, while Max Brand was a mediocre New York poet named Frederick Schiller Faust, who turned out implausible six-shooter tales from the terrace of an Italian villa).

Nevertheless, and needless to say, L. Ron Hubbard persevered and soon earned a reputation as among the most publishable names in pulp fiction, with a ninety percent placement rate of first-draft manuscripts. He was also among the most prolific, averaging between seventy and a hundred thousand words a month. Hence the rumors that L. Ron Hubbard had redesigned a typewriter for faster keyboard action and pounded out manuscripts on a continuous roll of butcher paper to save the precious seconds it took to insert a single sheet of paper into manual typewriters of the day.

That all L. Ron Hubbard stories did not run beneath said byline is yet another aspect of pulp fiction lore. That is, as publishers periodically rejected manuscripts from top-drawer authors if only to avoid paying top dollar, L. Ron Hubbard and company just as frequently replied with submissions under various pseudonyms. In Ron's case, the

A MAN OF MANY NAMES

Between 1934 and 1950, L. Ron Hubbard authored more than fifteen million words of fiction in more than two hundred classic publications. To supply his fans and editors with stories across an array of genres and pulp titles, he adopted fifteen pseudonyms in addition to his already renowned L. Ron Hubbard byline.

Winchester Remington Colt
Lt. Jonathan Daly
Capt. Charles Gordon
Capt. L. Ron Hubbard
Bernard Hubbel
Michael Keith
Rene Lafayette
Legionnaire 148
Legionnaire 14830
Ken Martin
Scott Morgan
Lt. Scott Morgan
Kurt von Rachen
Barry Randolph
Capt. Humbert Reynolds

list included: Rene Lafayette, Captain Charles Gordon, Lt. Scott Morgan and the notorious Kurt von Rachen—supposedly on the lam for a murder rap, while hammering out two-fisted prose in Argentina. The point: While L. Ron Hubbard as Ken Martin spun stories of Southeast Asian intrigue, LRH as Barry Randolph authored tales of

L. Ron Hubbard, circa 1930, at the outset of a literary career that would finally span half a century.

romance on the Western range—which, stretching between a dozen genres is how he came to stand among the two hundred elite authors providing close to a million tales through the glory days of American Pulp Fiction.

In evidence of exactly that, by 1936 L. Ron Hubbard was literally leading pulp fiction's elite as president of New York's American Fiction Guild. Members included a veritable pulp hall of fame: Lester "Doc Savage" Dent, Walter "The Shadow" Gibson, and the legendary Dashiell Hammett—to cite but a few.

Also in evidence of just where L. Ron Hubbard stood within his first two years on the American pulp circuit: By the spring of 1937, he was ensconced in Hollywood, adopting a Caribbean thriller for Columbia Pictures, remembered today as *The Secret of Treasure Island*. Comprising fifteen thirty-minute episodes, the L. Ron Hubbard screenplay led to the most profitable matinée serial in Hollywood history. In accord with Hollywood culture, he was thereafter continually called upon

The 1937 Secret of Treasure Island, *a fifteen-episode serial adapted for the screen by L. Ron Hubbard from his novel,* Murder at Pirate Castle.

to rewrite/doctor scripts—most famously for long-time friend and fellow adventurer Clark Gable.

In the interim—and herein lies another distinctive chapter of the L. Ron Hubbard story—he continually worked to open Pulp Kingdom gates to up-and-coming authors. Or, for that matter, anyone who wished to write. It was a fairly unconventional stance, as markets were already thin and competition razor sharp. But the fact remains, it was an L. Ron Hubbard hallmark that he vehemently lobbied on behalf of young authors—regularly supplying instructional articles to trade journals, guest-lecturing to short story classes at George Washington University and Harvard, and even founding his own creative writing competition. It was established in 1940, dubbed the Golden Pen, and guaranteed winners both New York representation and publication in *Argosy*.

But it was John W. Campbell Jr.'s *Astounding Science Fiction* that finally proved the most memorable LRH vehicle. While every fan of L. Ron Hubbard's galactic epics undoubtedly knows the story, it nonetheless bears repeating: By late 1938, the pulp publishing magnate of Street & Smith was determined to revamp *Astounding Science Fiction* for broader readership. In particular, senior editorial director F. Orlin Tremaine called for stories with a stronger *human element*. When acting editor John W. Campbell balked, preferring his spaceship-driven tales, Tremaine enlisted Hubbard. Hubbard, in turn, replied with the genre's first truly *character-driven* works, wherein heroes are pitted not against bug-eyed monsters but the mystery and majesty of deep space itself—and thus was launched the Golden Age of Science Fiction.

The names alone are enough to quicken the pulse of any science fiction aficionado, including LRH friend and protégé, Robert Heinlein, Isaac Asimov, A. E. van Vogt and Ray Bradbury. Moreover, when coupled with LRH stories of fantasy, we further come to what's rightly been described as the foundation of every modern tale of horror: L. Ron Hubbard's immortal *Fear*. It was rightly proclaimed by Stephen King as one of the very few works to genuinely warrant that overworked term "classic"—as in: *"This is a classic tale of creeping, surreal menace and horror. . . . This is one of the really, really good ones."*

L. Ron Hubbard, 1948, among fellow science fiction luminaries at the World Science Fiction Convention in Toronto.

To accommodate the greater body of L. Ron Hubbard fantasies, Street & Smith inaugurated *Unknown*—a classic pulp if there ever was one, and wherein readers were soon thrilling to the likes of *Typewriter in the Sky* and *Slaves of Sleep* of which Frederik Pohl would declare: *"There are bits and pieces from Ron's work that became part of the language in ways that very few other writers managed."*

And, indeed, at J. W. Campbell Jr.'s insistence, Ron was regularly drawing on themes from the Arabian Nights and

113

so introducing readers to a world of genies, jinn, Aladdin and Sinbad—all of which, of course, continue to float through cultural mythology to this day.

At least as influential in terms of post-apocalypse stories was L. Ron Hubbard's 1940 *Final Blackout*. Generally acclaimed as the finest anti-war novel of the decade and among the ten best works of the genre ever authored—here, too, was a tale that would live on in ways few other writers imagined.

Portland, Oregon, 1943; L. Ron Hubbard, captain of the US Navy subchaser PC 815.

Hence, the later Robert Heinlein verdict: "Final Blackout *is as perfect a piece of science fiction as has ever been written.*"

Like many another who both lived and wrote American pulp adventure, the war proved a tragic end to Ron's sojourn in the pulps. He served with distinction in four theaters and was highly decorated for commanding corvettes in the North Pacific. He was also grievously wounded in combat, lost many a close friend and colleague and thus resolved to say farewell to pulp fiction and devote himself to what it had supported these many years—namely, his serious research.

But in no way was the LRH literary saga at an end, for as he wrote some thirty years later, in 1980:

"Recently there came a period when I had little to do. This was novel in a life so crammed with busy years, and I decided to amuse myself by writing a novel that was pure *science fiction."*

114

That work was *Battlefield Earth: A Saga of the Year 3000*. It was an immediate *New York Times* bestseller and, in fact, the first international science fiction blockbuster in decades. It was not, however, L. Ron Hubbard's magnum opus, as that distinction is generally reserved for his next and final work: The 1.2 million word *Mission Earth*.

> **Final Blackout**
> *is as perfect a piece of science fiction as has ever been written.*
>
> —Robert Heinlein

How he managed those 1.2 million words in just over twelve months is yet another piece of the L. Ron Hubbard legend. But the fact remains, he did indeed author a ten-volume *dekalogy* that lives in publishing history for the fact that each and every volume of the series was also a *New York Times* bestseller.

Moreover, as subsequent generations discovered L. Ron Hubbard through republished works and novelizations of his screenplays, the mere fact of his name on a cover signaled an international bestseller. . . . Until, to date, sales of his works exceed hundreds of millions, and he otherwise remains among the most enduring and widely read authors in literary history. Although as a final word on the tales of L. Ron Hubbard, perhaps it's enough to simply reiterate what editors told readers in the glory days of American Pulp Fiction:

He writes the way he does, brothers, because he's been there, seen it and done it!

THE STORIES FROM THE GOLDEN AGE

Your ticket to adventure starts here with the Stories from
the Golden Age collection by master storyteller L. Ron Hubbard.
These gripping tales are set in a kaleidoscope of exotic locales and brim
with fascinating characters, including some of the
most vile villains, dangerous dames and brazen heroes
you'll ever get to meet.

The entire collection of over one hundred and fifty stories is being
released in a series of eighty books and audiobooks.
For an up-to-date listing of available titles,
go to www.goldenagestories.com.

AIR ADVENTURE

117

FAR-FLUNG ADVENTURE

The Adventure of "X"
All Frontiers Are Jealous
The Barbarians
The Black Sultan
Black Towers to Danger
The Bold Dare All
Buckley Plays a Hunch
The Cossack
Destiny's Drum
Escape for Three
Fifty-Fifty O'Brien
The Headhunters
Hell's Legionnaire
He Walked to War
Hostage to Death

Hurricane
The Iron Duke
Machine Gun 21,000
Medals for Mahoney
Price of a Hat
Red Sand
The Sky Devil
The Small Boss of Nunaloha
The Squad That Never Came Back
Starch and Stripes
Tomb of the Ten Thousand Dead
Trick Soldier
While Bugles Blow!
Yukon Madness

SEA ADVENTURE

Cargo of Coffins
The Drowned City
False Cargo
Grounded
Loot of the Shanung
Mister Tidwell, Gunner

The Phantom Patrol
Sea Fangs
Submarine
Twenty Fathoms Down
Under the Black Ensign

TALES FROM THE ORIENT

MYSTERY

FANTASY

SCIENCE FICTION

WESTERN

JOIN THE PULP REVIVAL
America in the 1930s and 40s

Pulp fiction was in its heyday and 30 million readers were regularly riveted by the larger-than-life tales of master storyteller L. Ron Hubbard. For this was pulp fiction's golden age, when the writing was raw and every page packed a walloping punch.

That magic can now be yours. An evocative world of nefarious villains, exotic intrigues, courageous heroes and heroines—a world that today's cinema has barely tapped for tales of adventure and swashbucklers.

Enroll today in the Stories from the Golden Age Club and begin receiving your monthly feature edition selected from more than 150 stories in the collection.

You may choose to enjoy them as either a paperback or audiobook for the special membership price of $9.95 each month along with FREE shipping and handling.

CALL TOLL-FREE: 1-877-8GALAXY
(1-877-842-5299) OR GO ONLINE TO
www.goldenagestories.com
AND BECOME PART OF THE PULP REVIVAL!